D0285012

THONGOR AGAINST THE GODS

A new ruler has arisen on the ancient continent of Lemuria. It is Thongor the Barbarian, whose dauntless courage and mighty sword have made him overlord of a thriving young empire.

Against him conspire in secret those dedicated to the Black Gods of Chaos.

Suddenly Thongor's wife, the Princess Sumia, is abducted. Thongor speeds to her rescue—but his enemies are cunning as well as ruthless. Embroiled deeper and deeper in a danger compounded of both sorcery and science, Thongor learns that he must carry his battle to the Gods themselves!

THONGOR
AGAINST
THE GODS

Lin Carter

WARNER BOOKS

A Warner Communications Company

THONGOR AGAINST THE GODS

is dedicated to all of Thongor's friends who
have been kind enough to write me, and especially to:
Lloyd Alexander and *Henry Mazzeo*

and to *Noel,*

with love and puppies.

WARNER BOOKS EDITION

Copyright © 1967 by Paperback Library, Inc.
All rights reserved.

ISBN 0-446-94178-6

Cover art by Kevin Johnson

Warner Books, Inc., 75 Rockefeller Plaza, New York, N.Y. 10019

Ⓦ A Warner Communications Company

Printed in the United States of America

First Printing: November, 1967

Reissued: August, 1979

10   9   8   7   6   5   4   3   2

Prologue

THE LEGEND OF THONGOR THE BARBARIAN

". . . It was an Age of Magic, when the might of Wizards strove against the tides of darkness that hovered over the Lands of Men like threatening wings. And the world shall not again see such wizardry as reigned of old when proud Lemuria was young, and ere the Mother of Empires spread her banners over Aegyptus, young Atlan, and the rose-red cities of the Maya-Kings. Into this violent age of sorcery and conquest, of the assassin's dagger and the venomed chalice, where the greed of Sark was set against the blood-lust of Druid, with the Throne of Lemuria for prize . . . came one man, a wandering adventurer from the savage wilderness of the Northlands: Thongor of Valkarth, armed with the iron thews of the warrior and the barbarian's contempt of danger. With the aid of the great wizard, Sharajsha, he overwhelmed the Dragon Kings and foiled their mighty plot to summon the Dark Gods of Chaos from beyond the farthest star. The first of these Lords of Darkness was Yamath, whose fiery altars he shattered, whose Yellow Druids he drove into exile, taking unto himself the throne of Patanga where Yamath had ruled. But two of the Black Gods remained unconquered: still bloody Slidith reigned in grim Tsargol, still the Red Druids held sway over the stone city by the southern sea . . ."

—The Lemurian Chronicles

This is the tale of Thongor's battle against the Gods.

Chapter 1

THE THIEF OF TSARGOL

Some men make war with whispered lies!
Sharp is the tongue, and swift to kill,
Keen as the dagger-blade that flies
From assassin's hand with coward's skill.
—*The Scarlet Edda*

Midnight hung like a black curtain over Tsargol. The walled city of red stone rose sheer from the southern shore of ancient Lemuria, where the cold waves of Yashengzeb Chun the Southern Sea broke in thunder against their cliffy height.

All was darkness. No light burned in the domes of towers, nor blazed along the mighty avenues. The magnificent palace of a thousand windows rose in a mountain of ebon blackness, for the last monarch of Tsargol was dead. Nor did lantern or candelabrum blaze in the Temple Quarter, where the Druids of Slidith dwelt, the wizard-priests of the savage and bloody cult that had ruled the red stone city unchallenged, since the death of Drugunda Thal, the last Sark.

The city was black as a city of the dead.

And as silent, save for the never-ending thunder of the surf, where the sea hurled itself in mindless fury against the great wall as it had done for a thousand years and would do for ten thousand more.

But all were not asleep on this black and starless night in seacoast Tsargol. In a small, square chamber cut from the granite upon which the city reared its crown of pinnacles and swelling domes, forty yards beneath the sacred Scarlet Tower of the Star Stone, four men in hooded robes of black velvet sat plotting about a massive table of crimson jade.

At this depth, they heard only the utter silence of eternity, for not even the remorseless sledge-hammer of the pounding surf could penetrate the enduring stone that walled them in. The chamber was lit by great candles set in an iron bracket on the table. Three candles, each as thick as a warrior's arm, shed a sickly, wavering light over the blood-red jade, and over the four faces.

At one end of the table sat the tall, lean figure of Yelim Pelorvis, the Red Archdruid, who ruled over Tsargol in the name of Slidith, the Lord of Blood. His stooped figure was wasted, gaunt, almost skeletal. His face was cold and thin, fleshless as a skull, with a shaven pate that gleamed in the flickering light as if it were a globe of polished ivory. His slitted eyes were colorless and without luster, their gaze turned inwards, like one lost in the grip of the deathly drug *nothlaj*, the Flower of Dreams.

He spoke in a thin, dull voice. "How shall we gain revenge over this Thongor, this gutter-whelp of a barbarian, who violated the sanctuary of the Lord Slidith and stole therefrom the Star Stone, that sacred talisman that fell from the skies over the Scarlet City a thousand years ago? The Lord Slidith hath spoken to me in my dreams, saying the Dark Lords demand the barbarian die. Speak!"

To the left of Yelim Pelorvis sat Numadak Quelm. He was a younger man, similarly shaven, and in his hard face burned eyes ablaze with the fiery madness of a fanatic. Beneath his robes of black velvet he wore the yellow satin of a priest of the outlawed cult of Yamath the Fire-God.

He spoke in a voice vibrant with hatred. "To me, as well, have the gods whispered as I lay in slumber, my astral body roaming the Shadowlands. The voice of Yamath spoke to me, bidding that the barbarian, Thongor, who slew my master the Yellow Archdruid Vaspas Ptol and who has mounted the throne of Yamath's sacred city, Patanga, with his bride the Princess Sumia, must die—else

8

the Three Lords of Chaos shall never regain empery over this planet! Thongor must be slain—but how?"

To the left of the outlawed Druid from Patanga sat a small, fat man whose shroud of ebon velvet hid garments of pretentious, gaudy hue, jeweled and brocaded fantastically. Within his toadlike, heavy-jowled face, small beady eyes gleamed malignantly. This was Arzang Pome, exiled Sark of Shembis, whose sadistic lust of cruelty made his name dreaded throughout the Southern Kingdoms. Him Thongor had overthrown and sent into wandering exile, replacing his bloody reign with that of Thongor's staunch comrade, young Ald Turmis.

Arzang Pome rubbed his fat, toadlike hands together, the gems of his many rings twinkling in the dim light. He said greedily, "The barbarian thrust me from my throne, what time I joined with Phal Thurid, Sark of Thurdis, and went up against Patanga in war! I say unleash against him the cunning of the Assassin's Guild—let a venomed goblet or a dagger from the shadows mark the end of this Northlander dog!"

The Yellow Archdruid of Patanga frowned. "Nay! A dagger is no better than the wrist of the assassin who wields it—venom no surer than the poisoner's skill! I say say let us summon the powerful aid of our brothers, the Black Druids of Zaar, who serve the Third Lord of Chaos! With the power of the great City of Magicians behind us, we can safely and surely strike down the Northlander with unerring magic."

The Red Archdruid shook his head. "Numadak Quelm, you are wrong. Zaar, the City of Magicians, lies a thousand leagues from my city of Tsargol, beyond the jungles and the forests and the endless eastern plains where the Blue Nomads roam and rule, beyond the Mountain of Doom, at the very edge of Lemuria. There is no time to summon a dark magic of death from the Black Brotherhood. Daily, the young empire of Thongor grows vaster and more powerful. Already the barbarian and his prin-

9

cess rule the Three Cities of Thurdis, Patanga and Shembis on the Gulf. At any time he may turn his savage eye southwards, upon Tsargol. We must strike now!"

The fourth member of this secret council had not yet spoken, sitting wrapped in his thoughts, the black cowl shrouding his face. Now he leaned forward into the wavering light of the three huge candles, and the hood fell back, exposing his features. He was tall, strongly built, clothed like a warrior in chainmail over a leathern surcoat. His face was tanned and strong; a grim black beard framed his hard, cruel mouth. His eyes were sharp, alert, intelligent. This was Hajash Tor, the conquered and banished Daotarkon or commander of the Host of Thurdis. He it was whose mad, uncontrolled ambition and dreams of conquest had goaded the weak-willed Sark of Thurdis on the scarlet road of empire. When Thongor had broken the Thurdan seige to his city of Patanga, Hajash Tor had fled, slaying the pitiful and craven king of Thurdis whom his wiles had led into this mad war.

He spoke. "There is yet another way, my Lord Archdruid, to bring doom upon Patanga and death to the barbarian. . . ."

Yelim Pelorvis turned dull eyes upon him. In his soft, colorless voice he said, "What way is that?"

Hajash Tor leaned forward, gathering the attention of the three other conspirators with a compelling glance of his keen, magnetic eyes. "I agree with Yelim Pelorvis that Patanga must be destroyed before its empire encompasses us here. Thongor is now building an aerial fleet of those flying ships of which Patanga alone hath the secret. The airboat is the deadliest of weapons, for armed with a single such flying craft, Thongor broke my seige of Patanga and defeated an entire army under my command. Right at this moment, my lords, is the hour to strike. Ere the year is out, Thongor will have completed his fleet and trained his flying warriors—and Patanga will be unconquerable, the most potently armed and most powerful city in all Lemuria. But Thongor must not be slain by an assassin—nor by magic."

"How then?" breathed the obese little ex-Sark of Shembis. A cruel smile touched the thin hard lips of Hajash Tor.

"To slay him swiftly would be to rob us of our vengeance," he said softly. "Death is an absolute end—but there are torments that can seem to last a thousand years of agony, before death ends them forever!"

His words fell one by one into the stifling silence of the secret underground chamber. His glittering eyes flashed with a leering glint of evil. In silence they pondered his words.

"How shall we bring Thongor into the reach of our torturers, Hajash Tor, from amidst his mighty army and from the heart of his walled and well-guarded city?" Yelim Pelorvis inquired.

Hajash Tor smiled again. "We shall make him come to us of his own free will," he said softly.

The young Archdruid of Yamath leaned forward, eyes glowing with fanaticism, wetting his lips eagerly. "How?"

Hajash Tor lowered his voice to a sly whisper.

"Suppose we were to steal from the heart of Thongor's palace, by secrecy and stealth, his mate, the Princess Sumia, and their newborn child, the Prince Tharth. One man can steal through a wall of guards, where an army would fail."

"Continue," the Red Archdruid said colorlessly.

"When Sumia and her child are safely within our walls, we can command Thongor—if ever he wishes to see his Sarkaja and their firstborn alive—to open the gates of Patanga to our army, to bid his men lay down their arms, and to deliver himself into our hands! Else, we shall destroy those he loves best."

Yelim Pelorvis contemplated the scheme with dull, thoughtful eyes, musingly. "Will he believe our messenger?"

11

Hellish mirth rang in the commander's voice. "We shall send him proof. Your torturers are skillful enough to cut off the Sarkaja's left hand and yet allow her to live. Our messenger shall bear this scarlet evidence to the gallant barbarian, where he sits enthroned in the midst of a thousand warriors. He will hasten to come to us, I warrant!"

The little toadlike Sark of Shembis giggled unnervingly—a terrible, gloating sound. "Where shall we find a man clever enough to accomplish this?"

Hajash Tor leaned back, relaxing, confident. "There is in this city of Tsargol a certain thief called Zandar Zan. . . ."

Two weeks later, a slim young man astride a dusty kroter rode through the great West Gate of Patanga at high noon. The sun blazed down on the flame-yellow walls of the mighty city, striking fire from the glazed tiles atop the conical-roofed towers, and catching a brazen gleam in the fat-bellied domes of gilded brass and green copper. The mighty gate loomed above him like a cliff, darkening the clear blue sky. Sun flashed gold from lancehead and helm of the guards stationed atop the wall. From a dozen tower tops, the cloth-of-gold banner of Patanga, now charged with the Black Hawk of Valkarth, snapped and fluttered in the fresh breeze.

The slim young man was unnoticed as he entered the city amidst a throng of people. There were merchants from Zangabal in white cloth caps topped with amber plumes, bearing goods of worked leather, brassware, and bright silken carpets from the looms of Dalakh and Cadorna. Pompous ambassadors from Kathool in the north came, borne in veiled palanquins, bearing gifts of gold, silver, and priceless jazite. Farmers from the outlying provinces came hither, riding to market in great wains drawn by immense, ponderous zamphs, with loads of fresh sarnberries and waterfruit, and wheat and corn from their fields. And with them came flocking dusty young swordsmen from distant Ashembar, archers and mounted spearmen from far Darundabar, and mercenaries from Vozashpa, drawn by the magic of the legend of Thongor, the mightiest of warriors, bravest and most generous of kings, to enlist in his growing armies or, perchance, to learn the mysterious arts of piloting the slim silvery airboats that floated and circled like enchanted ships high in the sparkling air over royal Patanga.

He passed through the towering West Gate and rode into the imperial city along the mighty Thorian Way, that great avenue that cut through the heart of the city to the magnificent square at Patanga's center. About him rose palaces and temples, mansions and marts—fabulous, rich with a thousand hues, glittering with barbaric grandeur.

Multicolored carpets and bright banners hung from balcony and window and wall; flags writhed and unfolded from minaret and spire. Superb façades of sculpture marble, dressed stone or dazzling mosaics caught the noontide sun. In the great Bazaar of Patanga, merchants squabbled and gesticulated beneath striped awnings of orange and blue and crimson. Green trees drooped beneath their freight of leaves, casting cool lakes of shade over the blistering pavement, and gardens of fantastic flowers could be glimpsed here and there between buildings.

The streets and avenues were filled with a brilliant throng—wives off to market, warriors bound for their posts, royal heralds in tabards of black-and-gold bearing scrolls and messages, priests of wise Father Gorm or gentle Lady Tiandra, lords and nobles in gilt-wheeled chariots or mounted on lean whip-tailed kroters, running boys on unknowable errands—but none noted the quiet-faced young man on the dusty kroter, in the faded and patched motley of a wandering troubadour, with an ivory lute slung over his back.

Zandar Zan (for of course it was he) turned off at the great bazaar onto a side street, and dismounted before a large inn called The Sign of the Dragon's Head and allowed a stable boy to lead his reptilian mount off to the pens.

He entered the inn and paid for a room for the night, ordering a tankard of sarn-wine and a roast haunch of bouphar meat from the innkeeper. And then he lay down on his bed and waited calmly for darkness to fall.

When night came, and the great golden moon of ancient Lemuria filled the skies with her light, Zandar Zan left the Dragon's Head muffled in a voluminous cloak of dull gray. He had exchanged his patched suit of motley for a peculiar skin-tight garment of dead black that clothed him like a glove from throat to wrist and heel, but this unusual raiment was concealed from notice by the hooded gray cloak. He moved through the well-lighted city, choosing dark alleys and obscure, little-traveled paths, coming at last to the wall that enclosed the palace of the Sarkon.

Awaiting a moment when the moon would be hidden behind a cloud, for it was a hot summer night and the sky was thick with vapors, he took refuge in the ink-black darkness of a huge flowering othlar tree. There he whisked off his gray cloak and swiftly turned it inside out. This cloak was lined with the same dead-black cloth his other garments were made of, and effectively hid him from sight. He next pulled a black mask over his face and drew, from a hidden pocket in the heavy cloak, a length of thin wire to whose end was fastened a collapsible many-pronged hook of black iron, its prongs sheathed in a layer of thick cloth to muffle the sound. When the moon slid behind a cloud, Zandar Zan hurled this grappling-hook over the walls of the royal enclosure. The prongs slid, gratingly, along the wall's top, then caught in the row of sharp spikes that were set in the stones to repel intruders. Swiftly and silently, the Black Thief of Tsargol clambered up the wall, detached the hooks, and leaped over into the dark gardens below.

The Palace of a Thousand Sarks was set in the midst of a splendid park—a maze of thick shrubbery, flowery gardens, and groves of incense-bearing trees, interspersed with small streams and lotus pools. Warriors of the Black Dragons—the Sarkon's own regiment of hand-picked guards—were stationed at various points amid the park; hidden from sight by his black garments, the thief glided through the dense bushes, finding it easy to elude the unsuspecting soldiers.

He came to a wall of the palace itself. If the maps he had studied in Tsargol were correct, this tower bore the private apartments of Thongor and Sumia. Wasting no time, Zandar Zan drew from a pouch a peculiar pair of harnesses which he slipped on over his boots, drawing them very tight. Keen spikes of nebium, strongest of all metals, protruded from these harnesses. Then he drew on special gloves to which similar spikes were affixed.

Then he walked up the wall.

Zandar Zan was no ordinary thief. He was the thief of all thieves: graceful and limber as an acrobat, tough-muscled as a gladiator, he possessed the skills of an assassin and the strength of a warrior. But even his amazing powers were strained to accomplish this weird feat.

The wall of the royal tower was built of vast blocks of smooth, glistening yellow marble. But between each block was a softer, spongier layer of cement. Into this dry, crumbling and porous substance, the master-thief first drove the sharp spikes on his wrists. Then, raising himself with agile strength, he drove his boot-spikes into the cement-layer between a lower block of marble. Now, balanced on the boot-spikes, he wrenched loose his wrist-spikes with a practised twist and drove them in again, still higher. Like some fantastic worm he inched his slow, exhausting way straight up the wall in this ingenious manner.

The Princess Sumia was alone in her suite, awaiting the

arrival of Thongor. Prince Tharth had just been fed by his nurse. The boy, only a year old, lay sleeping in a crib beside the great throne-like chair wherein the young and lovely Sarkaja of Patanga sat dreaming.

Tonight there were no state dinners, no festive banquets or balls. Tonight she and Thongor would dine alone in their apartments, just the two of them. She smiled softly at the thought. So heavy had been the affairs of the Three Cities that of late she and her beloved mate had scarce had an hour alone. But tonight was theirs to share and enjoy—theirs and their son's, for within moments Thongor would burst in shouting for wine and seize her up in a crushing embrace that would leave her breathless. He would close her smiling lips with a kiss that would leave her weak and shaken, and then he would release her and snatch up the boy. Thundering with deep-chested laughter, the Valkarthan would toss the delighted child into the air and catch him in strong, gentle arms while the princess watched their game with proud eyes. Soon . . .

But how swiftly her dream was torn from her.

That sound! The window——?

She turned at the unexpected clink of steel and screamed suddenly to see the cloaked and hooded figure, black and monstrous as some great bat, that stood within the huge open window, bending grim cold eyes upon her.

Sumia was on her feet in a flash, screaming for aid. But just as swiftly the terrible black form hurled itself upon her and she saw the deadly gleam of a naked steel blade in one black hand, darting towards her throat.

Chapter 2

PRINCESS IN PERIL

> Steel rings on steel—an iron song!
>   We hew our red path through the throng
> And with each stroke we break their line—
>   As drunk with battle as with wine!
>   —*The Battle-Song of the Black Dragons*

Thongor of Valkarth swung his mighty Northlander broadsword with the full strength of his giant thews behind each great stroke. His lips were drawn back, baring his teeth in a tigerish grin and the red joy of battle flamed in his strange golden eyes.

Steel met steel, ringing with war's grim music. Sparks flew as his opponent's blade shattered before the irresistible force of Thongor's blow. The man was half-driven to his knees, and raised his cherm to catch the return blow of the terrible longsword. The cherm, as the Lemurian shield was called, was a small, circular buckler strapped tightly to the left forearm. Tough, varnished dragonhide-leather stretched over a light frame of arld wood comprised this shield and one used it to adroitly catch and turn the glancing stroke of a sword, rather than to sustain the full force of a descending blade-edge.

The huge muscles of Thongor's naked shoulders writhed and knotted with the power of his return stroke. Its impact knocked the kneeling swordsman flying and left his cherm a tangle of smashed wood and torn leather.

Thongor planted his booted feet firmly and laughed as a comrade helped the fallen swordsman stagger to his feet.

"Well done, Charn Kojun! We shall make a Dragon of

you yet!" he boomed, clapping the younger man on the shoulder. Charn Kojun grinned, wincing.

"Aye, sire, if I manage to survive the training unslain!"

Thongor laughed, sheathing his broadsword. He accepted a great crimson cloak from a warrior and threw it about his brawny shoulders, drawing one end of the cloak under his arm and across his chest and fastening the garment to the shoulder-strap of his harness with a cairngorm brooch.

The mighty Valkarthan was an imposing figure—a bronzed giant of a man, thewed like a titan, broad-shouldered, deep-chested, narrow of waist and long of leg. His superb body was naked save for a black leather harness, girdle, scarlet loincloth and black buskins, or calf-high boots. His dark unruly mane of coarse straight hair was tossed back over his shoulders, held out of his eyes by a strap of leather across the brows.

After a long, weary day in the council chamber or meeting hall, he liked nothing more than to strip off the heavy robes of royal brocade and strap himself into a warrior's plain leather harness to spend an hour among his troops exercising in the courtyard of the palace. From the swordsmen of Patanga, the archers of Thurdis, and the wandering mercenaries from a dozen cities who came flocking to the banner of Thongor, he was slowly forging a superbly trained regiment of seasoned veterans, skilled in every art and craft of war. This personal troop of Royal Guards—the Black Dragons—were to be the nucleus around which a great army would slowly form in years to come. To the Black Dragons, Thongor was not only king and commander, but comrade, as well. To a man, they loved him and would go to their death defending him and his mate.

All too soon came sundown—Thongor could happily have exercised for hours more. His simple, barbarian life, during the long years he had brawled and wandered across the continent of Lemuria as bandit-chieftain, mercenary swordsman, assassin, thief, pirate and adventurer, made him more at home in the rude warrior's barracks than in the palace of a Sark. But for nearly two years now, a trick of destiny or whim of the Nineteen Gods had given him a place on the throne of Patanga beside the woman he loved. First as Sark of Patanga, and now as Sarkon of the Three Cities—overlord or High King of a vigorously growing young Empire. He shrugged, grinning. His uncomplicated Northlander philosophy bade him accept whatever came his way.

Waving goodnight to his men, he strode out of the courtyard arm in arm with the young exiled Prince of Tsargol, his staunch comrade, Karm Karvus. They entered the palace and parted, Karm Karvus, as Daotar or colonel of the newly-formed Air Guard, headed for the airboat field, while Thongor strode up the stairs towards the royal suite where his mate and their son awaited his coming. The great red cloak belling out behind him and flapping at his heels, he passed through richly ornate corridors and gorgeously appointed apartments and antechambers. The walls were hung with gilt banners or velvet tapestries stiff with silver wire. Rare incense rose in webs of blue vapor from pierced brass censers. Porcelain bowls of tiralons, the green roses of Lemuria, sweetened the air as he passed.

He was halfway down the hall leading to the royal suite when he heard Sumia scream.

A civilized man—which the giant Valkarthan most emphatically was not—would have wasted precious moments reacting to her cry, wondering what it meant, perhaps calling to her. But Thongor exploded into instantaneous action, for his were the hair-trigger-sensitive nerves of the savage, whose life ever hung on his alertness to the slightest sign of danger—a rustling leaf, the creak of a board, a scent, a shadow, a whisper.

In three great strides he was at the door, his hand grasping the latch. It was locked from within. A civilized monarch would have called the guard and waited for them to break it down—Thongor sprang backwards several paces and launched himself through the air at the door, like a pouncing tiger. In mid-air he swiveled, turning so his booted heels crashed into the door just above the lock with the full weight and impact of his giant body. The door exploded inward, showering the room with flying fragments of broken wood. Thongor landed on his feet, catlike, taking in the scene before him with one lightning glance.

Sumia, unconscious, her wrists and ankles bound with straps of hide, hung over an arm of the cloaked and batlike figure of a man in skin-tight black who hovered above the crib wherein young Prince Tharth squalled lustily, beating his tiny fat fists in the air. One black-gloved hand was extended to snatch up the babe.

A rumble of animal fury rising in his throat, Thongor hurled himself at the black-masked intruder. But Zandar Zan, too, moved with astonishing swiftness. Tossing the light weight of Princess Sumia over his shoulder, he abandoned the child and sprang into the window where he vanished from sight instantly, swallowed up in the darkness.

For a second, Thongor paused beside the crib. A swift, all-encompassing glance told him the babe was unharmed, merely startled.

Then, without thought or hesitation, Thongor leaped through the window after the black intruder and vanished.

Karm Karvus paused in the corridor to speak with an old friend, the grizzled, bluff and hearty Lord Mael, Baron of Tesoni, one of Thongor's closest friends and wisest counselors. They were discussing the forthcoming Council of Kings, when Thongor the Sarkon would meet with and consult Ald Turmis, Sark of Shembis, and the old warrior, Barand Thon, Sark of Thurdis, over the problems and affairs of the Sarkonate. Thus he was only a few floors beneath the level of the suite and could hear Sumia's cry, the explosion as Thongor smashed in the door, and Thongor's own bellow of savage rage clearly.

Snatching their swords from their scabbards, Karm Karvus and Lord Mael raced up the stairs and arrived at the shattered door to the royal suite only moments after Thongor had hurtled out of the tower window. Guards from the corridors beyond came running, together with certain noble ladies who waited on the princess—among them, a dark, lovely young girl, Mael's own daughter, Inneld.

The bluff old Baron's deep voice cut through the babble of questions. "Daughter! What has happened here? Where is your mistress?"

Inneld lifted frightened eyes. "I know not, Father! I but left the room for a moment, to see if dinner was prepared and ready, for we expected momently the coming of my lord. The Lady Sumia was alone in this room with Prince Tharth—I heard her cry out——"

Karm Karvus sprang across the room to peer out of the open window. He looked up, then shouted, "Sumia's floater—it's taking off from the landing stage on the roof! By the Gods—someone is carrying off the Princess!"

Thongor dove through the window into pitch-black night, and his out-stretched hand met a dangling line, which he seized in an iron grip. Thirty feet below his heels, the night-shrouded garden wheeled as he strove to cling to the slender line. He could not know it, but when the Black Thief, climbing the outer wall of the tower, had gained the window-ledge, he had removed his grappling hook from beneath his cloak and flung it above to catch on the rooftop of the spire and provide a means of exiting with the princess and her child. Surprised by Thongor's sudden entrance, Zandar Zan had abandoned the prince and fled through the window, climbing the line to the roof with the swiftness and skill of an acrobat, unhampered by Sumia's light weight.

Looking up, Thongor saw a cloaked, batlike figure above, clambering over the edge of the roof. He glimpsed the pale gleam of Sumia's form over the shoulders of the black intruder. Teeth bared in a fighting snarl, Thongor began climbing the thin line. He went up hand over hand and gained the roof only moments after the thief. There he saw a terrible sight.

The roof of the tower had been converted to a landing stage for Patanga's new air-fleet. Moored to a mast, Sumia's own floater drifted at the end of its anchor-cable. As Thongor hauled himself over the ledge, he saw the masked figure climb aboard the airboat with Sumia and cast off the line. As weightless as a cloud, due to its gravity-resisting hull of urlium, the magic metal, the slim craft was set adrift on the air-currents of the night-winds.

Thongor crouched, then sprang into the air. The coiled muscles in his long legs thrust him in a high leap, propelling him like powerful springs. One hand brushed the deck-rail of the floater—slipped, then clung.

Dangling by the fingertips of one hand, he hung from the airboat as it drifted out over the palace.

Zandar Zan had planned to escape from Patanga by means of a stolen floater, and had prepared for this. Before leaving Tstargol, he had listened to Hajash Tor while the former Daotarkon explained how to pilot the mysterious flying ships. As commander of the host of Thurdis, Hajash Tor was knowledgeable in this art, for it had been old Oolim Phon, the wise alchemist of Thurdis, who had isolated urlium, the antigravitic metal, and who had invented the airboat as a secret weapon in Thurdis' plans to conquer the whole of Lemuria with a flying navy. Hence the Black Thief wasted no time. Racing across the deck, he entered the pilot's cabin and deposited Sumia on one of the two bunks that lined the two walls. Within seconds he had the vessel under control and steered it out over the city, unaware that Thongor still clung to the rail.

Then came the rasp of metal on metal from the deck behind him. Zandar Zan looked over his shoulder, to see Thongor—eyes blazing with fury—climbing over the rail onto the deck.

The Black Thief had not earned his title gratuitously. He was famed for quickness of thought and agility of mind. One black-gloved hand flashed out and turned the floater's wheel a half-turn to the left. The airboat responded to this touch on the controls by swerving violently, half over-turning for a moment. As its deck swung from a horizontal to a vertical plane, Thongor was taken off-balance and fell over the rail, hurtling into the night.

Zandar Zan smiled grimly and seized the controls, righting the craft. The powerful twin rotors in the rear of the hull whined as their keen blades bit savagely into the cold night air. Picking up speed, the floater sped like a glittering silvery arrow into the darkness. Within moments the slim craft had arrowed high above the walls and was hurtling into the south, while the domes and towers of Patanga dwindled and were lost far behind.

Thongor fell, whirling head over heel, through darkness. Then one clutching hand brushed against a pole, clung, and he dangled above one of the rooftops of the city, gasping for breath.

A young warrior ran towards him across the roof, shouting, naked blade flashing in his hand. From his silver-gilt harness and sparkling silver helmet, he was one of the newly-formed Air Guard. Thongor dropped to the roof, looking around. By the whim of the Gods, Zandar Zan had pitched him off only a few yards above this tower roof, which was also a landing stage. And there, only a few strides away, floated an airboat of the guard, tethered to the mooring mast which had broken his fall. He relaxed a little, grinning.

The warrior came up to him, saluting, his face pale. "Sire! What——"

"No time to talk," Thongor growled. He swung up the line onto the airboat's deck, and shouted, "Inform Prince Karm Karvus I go to follow the princess' floater—*southwards*. Have him summon the Air Guard to follow me—quickly now, lad! Cast off, there!"

The young warrior saluted and cast off the tether. The floater drifted free of the landing stage and, as Thongor sprang to the controls, its rotors whined into life and the second boat sped into the night only a few minutes behind the first. Soon the lights of Patanga vanished behind and the nighted landscape of farmlands and forests raced past under the keel of Thongor's craft.

Those few minutes, however, proved essential. Both floaters were of new, improved design with stronger motive power and capable of far swifter flying speed than Thongor's old ship, the *Nemedis*, which had been the original prototype of the new air fleet. Zandar Zan's craft had the advantage of a few minutes' flying time at top speed, and Thongor's craft trailed behind as it accelerated to a matching velocity. The two air boats flashed through the night sky, nor could the efforts of Zandar Zan widen the gap between them, any more than Thongor's skill could narrow this gap. Spaced equally apart, they shot through the cloudy darkness. Soon they were beyond the borders of Patanga and flying over the grassy hills and great forestlands of Ptartha.

The clouds, which had hidden the moon over Patanga, were fewer in these southern skies. Casting an anxious glance behind him, Zandar Zan could clearly see the pursuing airboat behind him. He did not know, of course, that Thongor of Valkarth was piloting the floater; he assumed, without much thought, that the alarm had gone up and one cruising ship of the aerial patrols was chasing

24

him. But regardless of the pilot, he must somehow contrive to throw the enemy off his trail. It would never do to lead him straight to Tsargol, thus giving the enemy advance warning of the preparations for war, and clear knowledge that the capture of the princess had been a Tsargolian plot.

He gazed around desperately, searching the sky for some means of throwing this flying hound off his scent. There to the east he saw a great bank of clouds building up over the lands of Nianga. On the far horizon he could dimly make out a mass of low mountains that must be the Ardath range. He swung the wheel sharply over, and headed east. There, in the vast continent of thick clouds that hung over Nianga, he hoped to evade pursuit.

Sumia slowly regained her senses. The black figure she had seen in the window had sprung upon her and knocked her unconscious. Now, awakening slowly, she looked about her and saw that she lay upon one of the two bunks in the cabin of an airboat, which, from the accouterments of the cabin, she recognized as her own personal floater.

There, hunched over the controls, was the cloaked and masked figure that had attacked her. Sumia realized some unknown enemy must have arranged to kidnap her —and perhaps her child as well. A glance around the compact little cabin, however, dissolved her fears on that count, for the little prince was nowhere to be seen. She attempted to rise, but sank back, her wrists and feet bound. For what terrible purpose had she been thus spirited off in the night? For a moment her senses reeled in sick panic. But she was no pampered weakling of a metropolitan civilization. Only a few generations of urban life lay between her and the barbaric savagery of her forebears. Grimly summoning her inner resources of courage, Sumia began to think coolly and calmly, seeking a way out of her predicament. She had no doubt but that her cry of surprise had been heard by alert, loyal guards. Doubtless by now all of Patanga was ringing with alarm and indignation. Perhaps swift ships of the Air Guard were winging after to recover her at this very moment. They could not help her escape from this predicament—even mighty Thongor could not help her at this moment. She must help herself!

For a moment her heart ached with longing for the protection of the warrior she loved. If only he was here at this instant, to shield her with his fighting strength and godlike courage! But, resolutely, she put such thoughts away. Thongor was *not* here, and she must act as he would in such a predicament—coolly, swiftly, boldly. She searched her agile wits for a way out of this situation, her small jaw squaring with determination.

As of yet, her masked abductor was unaware she had awakened. This was an advantage, however slight. And Thongor had taught her that when in danger, one must seize every advantage, however small, and use it to the fullest. Thus she began to plan, her intelligent and courageous mind seeking each conceivable avenue to safety.

With her hands bound behind her back, she was virtually helpless. However, she was not tied to the bunk. And her hands were bound only at the wrists. It might be possible to work about so that her hands were in front of her—thus, even though still bound, of some use. Twisting her young limbs with supple grace, Sumia doubled up her legs, folding them so that with some slight effort she might pass her bound wrists past her legs. Straightening, she now had her hands in front of her. And her eye caught the glint of polished steel: a dagger and a sword swung at the black waist of the mysterious kidnapper. *Perhaps* . . . .

Sumia sat up and slid her legs over the edge of the bunk. It was not easy to rise to her feet and to stand with her ankles bound within the swaying cabin of the floater, but she managed it. Then she began inching across the cabin floor.

Every lurch of the hurtling craft threatened to knock her off her balance, but with infinite effort she managed to cross the cabin without falling or being heard.

Now she stood directly behind the black-cloaked pilot, whose full attention was riveted on the cloudbank directly ahead of the speeding airboat. If she attempted to draw the man's dagger with her bound hands, her clumsiness would doubtless betray her and he would be able to seize her hands before she could drive the dagger into his body. For a moment courage failed within her young heart—bound as she was, how could her small strength avail against this man?

Then, seizing the reins of her courage stoutly, she reached out desperately, seized his head in her hands, and, before he could move or turn, with every atom of strength she could summon she slammed his head into the steel guard-rail that ran about the front windows of the cabin.

He crumpled over the controls, bleeding through his black mask. Zandar Zan was knocked out cold. With numb fingers she fumbled at the mask and tore it away. She had half-suspected she might recognize some old enemy, but this young man was a complete stranger to her.

Then she bent and snatched his dagger from its sheath of black leather. Sitting down on the bunk, she slid the handle of the dagger between her tightly bound ankles, thus holding the knife rigid. Then, slowly, patiently, she began to saw the bonds on his wrists against the keen blade. No time was to be lost; no matter that, within mere moments, her numb hands began to ache from this unusual strain. The kidnapper might regain his senses at any moment. Bound as she was, she could not defend herself against him—but, with her wrists free and a naked blade in her hand, she was willing to fight.

Thus engaged, Sumia was unaware as the airboat, now out of control, plunged into the thick cloudbank over Nianga and hurtled through the smothering vapors at the invisible Mountains of Ardath directly ahead.

Chapter 3

THE UNDERGROUND PALACE

> . . . Beyond the trackless jungles and beneath the mountain's base, there lay the secret fortress of the Wizard of the West. There the ancient sorceror, through the endless centuries of his immortality, sought in forbidden books and curious rites, the hidden secrets of Futurity. . . .
>
> —*The Third Book of Psenophis*

Dawn broke over Patanga, putting an end to the troubled turmoil of the night. Karm Karvus, who had not slept nor rested, summoned a council in the first hours of dawn. The palace was a scene of confusion—officers and nobles hurrying hither and thither, messengers bearing reports and orders, squads of warriors racing to man their posts. Thongor had not returned, nor had the far-ranging floaters of the air fleet found a trace of the stolen princess.

To the council came the leaders of the Sarkdom: Lord Mael, his grizzled lion's mane disheveled, his brow lined with worry; stout, red-faced old Baron Selverus, who had served Sumia's father, the late Sark, and who now lent his loyal devotion to her mate, Thongor; and Prince Dru, lean, witty, sardonic—but now his mocking jests were still, and unwonted soberness marked his gallant demeanor. Hither, too, came wise old Eodrym, the Archpriest of Father Gorm and Hierarch of the Temple of

28

Nineteen Gods, to lend his sagacity to these desperate councils.

Karm Karvus wasted no time on idle ceremony. He opened the council with a concise and pointed survey of the events of the previous night. "Our council, then, is confronted with a threefold problem. Where is the Sarkaja Sumia—who has stolen her and for what grim end? Where is our Lord Thongor, and how does he fare? And to what coming danger are these curious events a prelude?"

"In other terms, Karm Karvus," Prince Dru interrupted, "does the kidnapping of the princess mean an act of war against us by some as yet unnamed nation, or was it but a stroke of malice and revenge on the part of a single enemy?"

"Correct, Prince. What precautions could be taken, I have already put into action," Karm Karvus continued. "The alarm has been given: the guards are trebled, exerting fullest alertness. The Air Guard is still searching the surrounding country. Heralds have been dispatched in the swiftest airboats to bear the alarm to Ald Turmis in Shembis and old Barand Thon in Thurdis, bidding them be on watch."

"Gorm's Blood—begging your pardon, my Lord Archpriest!—you think then, lad, the stealing of the princess was but prologue to an invasion—an act meant to disrupt and panic us, so that Patanga might be thrown off balance and taken all the easier for the confusion and breakdown in morale?" Lord Mael rumbled. Karm Karvus nodded grimly. The old baron of Tesoni swore sulphurously. "The treacherous, sneaking worms! To war on women!"

Selverus growled, "But what foe have we, with Thurdis and Shembis whelmed and occupied by our staunchest friends? Surely not Zangabal or Pelorm—nor even Kathool to the north! They have exchanged embassies with us, and know they have naught to fear from Thongor."

Karm Karvus agreed. "Aye, Lord Selverus, but we have filled half of Lemuria with disgruntled enemies—the

Druids of Yamath whom Thongor exiled—who well may have settled in some nearby realm and there slyly provoked the slumbering ambitions of an otherwise friendly monarch."

Mael rubbed his bearded cheeks thoughtfully. "Aye, lad," he rumbled, "and there is ever Tsargol to the south. That city and its Red Brotherhood of the foul demon-god, Slidith, *they* have not forgotten the insult Thongor hurled in their teeth when he stole into the Tower of Woman-Headed Serpents and thieved away the Star Stone from under their noses! Nay—no more than they have forgiven him for escaping from their arena of punishment, slaying the Sacred Zemadar—*and* the Sark of Tsargol, Drugunda Thal, himself!"

"Perhaps," conceded Prince Dru. "Yet Tsargol lieth leagues and leagues away, beside the waters of Yashengzeb Chun the Southern Sea. I think we would best look for an enemy closer to home . . . some small city, fearful of the swift-growing power of Patanga, imagining a threat to its own sovereignty, and perhaps tempted by the exiled and revengeful Druids of Yamath. But whoever our enemy is, the question remains: what further can we do to protect our realm at this time?"

The wise old priest, who had listened thoughtfully to the discussion thus far, lifted his sacerdotal scepter tipped with a great storm-stone.

"My Lords, and young Karm Karvus?"

The Prince of Tsargol turned to the old man gratefully. "Aye, Father Eodrym? I had hoped you would lend us the wisdom of your years on these grave matters. Let us hear your thoughts!"

The priest chuckled. "The accumulation of years to one's head do not always add wisdom to his thoughts. However, I can offer one suggestion——"

They encouraged him to speak. So the old man rose, tall and impressive with his hoary beard and simple robes of white velvet. The ruddy light of morning, streaming through the tall, open windows of the council-hall, drew sparkling fires from the jeweled Wheel of Gorm that hung upon his chest from a chain of iron.

"My thoughts are these: with the alarm given, the patrols out, and messengers sent to our sister cities, we have done all that we may do in the defense of Patanga until our unknown enemy shall deign to reveal his face and name with some overt and hostile gesture. However, if there be aught we can do to reveal our enemy's name and purpose now, before he is ready to strike, we should be wise to do it."

"Agreed, Father Eodrym," Karm Karvus demanded, "but how?"

"To the west, across the great jungles of Chush and beneath the vast mountains, lieth the subterranean castle of the great wizard of Lemuria, Sharajsha himself, who leagued with Thongor and yourself, Karm Karvus, to overthrow the Dragon Kings two years ago and more, and on whose deep friendship for the Valkarthan warrior-king I think we can rely for assistance. . . ."

Within the hour one small, lone airboat rose from the landing stages and soared high above Patanga. It circled the city once, then pointed its sharp prow to the north and west and flew like some fantastic metallic bird into the morning sky.

At the controls in the small cabin sat Karm Karvus, his lean, powerful body naked save for the silvery leather harness of the Air Guards, and a great blue cloak thrown back over his bronzed shoulders. Eodrym had been right, of course: to whom else should they turn in this extremity, but to the mighty magician of Mommur?

Patanga lay at the mouth of the Saan. North, the Twin Rivers broke apart, the Saan curving north and east towards Kathool of the Purple Towers, the Ysar winding north and west through the savage jungles of Chush. Karm Karvus, in the swiftest floater he could find, now sped high in the clear sky, following the glistening silver ribbon of the Ysar as it wove a pale, glittering thread through the emerald tapestry of the thick jungles far below.

On the north horizon the vast mountain range of Mommur lifted into his view above the curve of the earth. Like a stupendous wall of solid stone, the Mountains of Mommur crossed the center of Lemuria from the borders of Pasht in the farthest west to the Inner Sea of Neol-Shendis a thousand leagues to the east.

Like an enormous arrow of mirror-bright urlium, the airboat clove the fresh morning sky with breathtaking speed. Slowly the tropic sun of prehistoric Lemuria ascended the doom of heaven to the zenith of noon. Just as slowly, it glided down the west as the shadows of late afternoon darkened the tangled green jungles far below. Ever the mountains loomed closer. Here and there among the mighty peaks that lifted into the air ten and twenty thousand feet above the surface of the continent, Karm Karvus could spy smoking craters. Several mountains gushed torrents of liquid fire and hurled dense plumes of inky vapor high into the atmosphere. For this was a dubious and frightening land, shaken by terrific earthquakes, torn by volcanic explosions of stupendous force . . . eloquent testimony to the continent-shattering powers that but slumbered, as yet, deep in the cavernous heart of Lemuria, but which would someday waken in thunder, to split the unstable land and sink all of ancient Lemuria beneath the primeval Pacific, as even now prophets and oracles warned.

The western sky was a crimson furnace of sunset as the airboat drifted down beside a mighty cliff that reared its wall of unbroken rock beside the edge of the jungle. Karm Karvus anchored his craft securely to the soaring, crimson trunk of a gigantic lotifer tree. From here he advanced on foot into a labyrinthine canyon that clove a deep gorge between two walls of towering rock. Clambering over masses of shattered stone, the young warrior ventured into a winding alley lined by stupendous cliffs, ending at last in a massive slab of solid stone that blocked his path. Thus far the Tsargolian could come unaided—but no further. He knew not the magic key that would unlock the grim gate to the wizard's underground palace. He could but hope that the enchanter's vigilance had noted his approach . . . *ah!*

Soundlessly the gigantic slab of rock sank into the earth. Before him the black mouth of a cavern yawned. He strode forward fearlessly into the blackness.

He stood in a place of fantastic and unearthly grandeur. All about the enormous cavern stretched, lit here and there by pools of smoldering sulphur and streams of hissing lava that cast a weird orange-scarlet light over a panorama of terrifying splendor. From the arched roof of the cave, dripping stalactites hung like the fangs in the jaw of some incredible dragon. And the cavern floor rose to meet them in glassy pinnacles of mineral deposited over countless aeons of geologic time by the slow, calcareous drippings. Karm Karvus made his way through this forest of stalagmites towards a distant wall of smoke under-lit by a deep crimson glow.

He emerged from the stone forest at the brink of a river of living flame. Here a sluggish trickle of molted lava had cut a deep channel through the floor of the cavern. The slow fluid glowed cherry-red, casting a blistering heat on Karm Karvus' naked body. Small, flickering yellow flames danced across the wrinkled, mud-like surface of the river of lava. Oily steam rose from it, making his eyes water.

A natural bridge arched over the flaming river, and by this arch of rock Karm Karvus made precarious passage of the lava-stream that guarded the secret gate to Sharajsha's palace like a moat of liquid fire.

On the other side of the lava stream, the cavern floor lifted into a broad, shallow porch of seven steps that led to a great door of rust-red iron, three times taller than a man's full height. To either side of this door stood crude gryphons of stone, rough rock claws spread and raised in menace, stony beaks open in a rigid, silent scream of warning. Set like eyes within their birdlike stone heads, smoky gray crystals glittered with yellow fires. Suppressing a shudder, Karm Karvus wondered if that yellow flicker was but the glassy reflection of the lava-light, or a strange magical half-life.

He mounted the shallow flight of seven steps and stood before the great iron door. With a groan of rusty hinges, the leaves of this portal yawned open before him to the touch of invisible hands.

Before him lay a long hall. At the further end of this mighty hall, hewn from the eternal stone of the mountain's heart, a dais of seven steps rose against a sheer wall, and upon this dais stood a throne-like chair of black marble. The chair was empty. A huge table of ancient wood ran the length of the hall. Candelabra of solid gold stood at either end of the table, but their candles were unlit and the weird room was shrouded in evil darkness—save for a hovering, flickering shape of pure white flame no larger than a human head!

Karm Karvus cried an oath, clutching at his sword as the nape-hairs lifted at his neck.

The weird flame-thing hovered in mid-air at the height of a man's heart, unsupported by aught that the prince could see. Primal night-fears flickered through Karm Karvus's brain, but then——

An eery whispering voice spoke from the dancing ball of white fire. "Fear not, Prince of Tsargol! My Master bids you welcome to his palace, and requires that you follow me to the chamber wherein he lieth awaiting you."

"Follow *you?*" Karm Karvus cried. "What—*are*—you?"

Was there a hint of inhuman mockery, a whisper of uncanny laughter in the sibilant voice? "Fear not, I say—here you are welcome! I am but an Elemental Spirit of Fire, bound to the service of the Wizard Sharajsha. Come, Prince Karm Karvus!"

34

Stifling his superstitious fears, the young warrior followed the fire-elemental through a doorway from the hall. It danced before him like the will-o'-the-wisp that often leads travelers astray in miasmic swamps and desolate waste. He strode after the weird globe of phosphorescent flame, through curious apartments filled with marvels. The walls were hung with tapestries whereon woven trees tossed and bent to magic winds—frescoes of strange art, whereon painted faces leered and smiled to see him pass —through doorways whose entablatures were supported by bearded, serpent-footed caryatids of carved brown marble, whose stone eyes turned to observe him as he went by.

Karm Karvus and his curious guide came at last into a great room raftered with beams of ancient wood wherefrom hung strange things—the skeleton of a man, fully articulated with golden wire—a stuffed corkodrill with rubies for eyes—bundles and clusters of pungent herbs and weirdly twisted roots. Against one wall, in a fireplace of glistening black marble, a magic emerald-green fire blazed, fed by no coals or woods. Another wall was covered with shelves whereon books were stacked, or leaned against each other—books, and yet more books—more than Karm Karvus had ever seen. Some were bound in worked leather, others were held between plates of metal: gold, silver, electrum, jazite, copper. Some books were covered with plates of unfamiliar wood, carved with grotesque and terrible runes and cryptoglyphs. Others resided between intricate covers of ivory, studded with winking rubies that glittered balefully, like the scarlet eyes of serpents. There were, as well, great scrolls and rolls of parchment stuffed into the shelves, and in the nooks and crannies between the leaning, tumbled volumes were flasks of colored powders, jars of nameless fluids, urns of weird drugs and frightful acids. Against the other walls lay long, low tables of porcelain and steel, whereon stood instruments of alchemical science—retorts and bowls and beakers, aludels and cupels, uncouth alembics and weirdly-shapen curcubits and athanors—whose purposes were mysteries to the young warrior.

Trapped within a mirror of polished silver, a captive ghost wavered like a green shadow. Suspended in a crystal vat of cloudy fluid, a human brain pulsed with a terrible semblance of life. But Karm Karvus barely noticed these things—his eye flashed at once to the old man who sat in a great high-backed chair of purple jannibar wood, drawn before a vast table of pale green jade, upon which lay open before him a book whose vellum pages were covered with painted pictograms worked in inks scarlet, black and gold.

"My Lord Sharajsha—what do you do?" he cried. Smiling, the old man lifted one gaunt hand, whose waxen pallor made it almost transparent.

"I *die*, Karm Karvus," he said in a gentle, tranquil voice.

In truth, the years lay heavily on him. His form was so wasted, his long-sleeved robes of neutral gray seemed to clothe a skeleton, not a living man. His great beard and mane were white as that virgin snow wherein the mountain peaks are clad. His face was lined and weary, pallid as wax, like his thin hands. But life still blazed in his black, magnetic eyes. There the unquenchable curiosity and mighty intellect of the greatest wizard of all Lemuria still burned with undiminished force. Karm Karvus shook his head in despair.

"Not you, Lord!"

"And why not I, as much as any man?" the old wizard asked gently. "True, I have extended my life for centuries through magic—but if even the eternal mountain wears away at last, through unnumbered millenia of wind and rain, unto a grain of dust—and the everlasting stars themselves grow old, after cycles of aeons beyond telling, and die like coals that flicker and smolder for a time, then turn to dead ash—why should not death claim even me, Sharajsha, in its eventual hour? I regret it not, Karm Karvus, for

36

life has afforded me much—my arts have plumbed into those secret places where Time and the Gods conceal their profoundest keys—and from this wisdom have I learned that everything that is, must someday pass!"

Karm Karvus bowed his head, numb with sorrow.

"But come, let us not waste what few hours remain to me—surely you have come here upon some dark mission, or in urgent need of my skills. Speak: how doth my good friend, Thongor, on his new-won throne? And his fair wife?"

With swift economy of words, Karm Karvus outlined the events of recent issue. When he was finished, Sharajsha regarded him with grave, melancholy eyes.

"I shall search into this, Karm Karvus, but now leave me for a time—follow yonder Fire Elemental into a more comfortable apartment, where I shall command food and drink for thee. Refresh and rest, and I shall summon thee again."

As the golden moon rose over ancient Lemuria, Karm Karvus rejoined the old sorcerer who bade him seat himself upon a bench. Sharajsha stared into the shadows with thoughtful eyes.

"This much have I discovered by arcane methods. Thy enemy is thine own city of Tsargol, where Numadak Quelm and Hajash Tor and Arzang Pome are leagued with the Red Archdruid to raise war against Patanga. It is a certain thief of Tsargol they have set to kidnap Sumia Sarkaja, yet their plans have gone awry and chance has carried the princess far into the east where curious dangers await both her and her mate, Thongor, who followeth after."

"Tsargol!" Karm Karvus swore. "Lord Mael of Tesoni did guess as much! Then Thongor and Sumia are still alive and—safe?"

Sharajsha mused. "Alive—but not safe. New dangers

threaten them among unfamiliar peoples of the east. Thou canst not be of help to them, Karm Karvus, but must be on guard lest the host of Tsargol set Patanga under seige."

"I shall return at once to Patanga and lead the air fleet in attack upon Tsargol!"

"Aye, it were wise to strike now, before thine foe is ready . . . and yet I see some danger lurking in Tsargol, some weapon potent enough to destroy thy fleet . . . what it is, my arts cannot quite make out. Be wary, then, and on thy guard!"

"I shall, my Lord Sharajsha, and my thanks for this most timely warning!" He rose to leave.

"Stay but a moment more, Karm Karvus!" With one feeble hand the old enchanter pointed to a great parchment book bound in emerald-green dragonhide. "It may be I shall never live to see thee or any of my friends again. Take then this book, my Testament and Grimoire, unto Patanga and place it there among the chiefest treasures of the realm. In times to come and ages yet unborn, a prince of Lemuria will have great need of it, or so I read the dim vistas of futurity!"

"I shall do this," the warrior promised.

"Yet one thing more, my young friend," Sharajsha said, passing a trembling hand over his weary brow. "Somewhere in all this matter are implicated the Black Druids who worship Thamungazoth, the Dark Lord of Magic. This Black Brotherhood dwelleth far and far to the east, in Zaar, the City of Magicians. It may be that danger threatens from distant Zaar not yet, but in the future . . . my eyes are old, my sight is dim . . . but I fear me a dark and terrible shadow gathereth in the eastern skies, which may extend its black wings over bright Patanga. It was from Zaar the Black City that I came hither to this cavern ages ago, for I revolted against the Black Druids and their unholy quest for dominion and power. When thou seest Thongor again, tell him to beware the Black City . . . and to remember, when darkness threatens, only one force can dispel it. . . ."

Through the black night Karm Karvus sped in his airboat, bearing to Patanga the last warning of the wizard of Lemuria. . . .

Chapter 4

THE MOUNTAIN OF DOOM

Beware the Black Mountain
The Gods have abandoned,
Lest doom overtake thee
And Death strike thee down.
—*Testament of Yaa*

Hunched over the controls, Thongor stared grimly through the glass pane of the floater's cabin, his burning gaze following the distant fleeing sliver of metal ahead with the fixed and burning ferocity of some great jungle cat. Indeed, his features bore a striking resemblance to those of the savage vandar, the mighty black lion of ancient Lemuria, with his unshorn mane of coarse black hair, the grim immobility of his features, and his strange catlike eyes, which were like twin disks of blazing gold flame.

His complete attention was focused on the distant airboat far ahead. In the darkness of the cloudy night, he could but dimly make out the other craft by the faint glimmer of light reflected along the curve of its mirror-bright hull. Deep within his breast, a savage fury consumed him, gnawing at his heart. But the grim-faced barbarian did not allow his fears for the safety of his beloved mate to divert his attention or occupy his thoughts: with every atom of skill he possessed he labored to wring yet another erg of speed from his hurtling craft.

It seemed as if he had bent over the floater's controls for hours now. His body ached with strain, with the unrelieved weariness of tense muscles. He had been puzzled to see the fleeing craft angle sharply into the east some time ago, for to his knowledge, the giant Valkarthan had no enemies in that portion of Lemuria, but still he followed its flight with grim, unwavering attention.

The two ships, that of the Princess Sumia and her mysterious captor, Zandar Zan, and the craft of Thongor which followed close behind, sped on through the black night like twin arrows of glistening silver. The dense forests of Ptartha flew past beneath them and soon they were hurtling over the land of Nianga, a wilderness-land wherein few men dwelt and few cities stood, since the Nineteen Gods Who Rule The World had smote this realm with Their curse four thousand years before, and the Gray Fog of Death had swept the earth clean of men and their unholy and blasphemous crime against the Gods.

Ahead of the pursued and the pursuer rose like a mighty wall the Ardath Mountains, still hundreds of leagues distant. And between the airboats and the mountains a vast area of dense vapors obtruded. Into this impenetrable region of mists plunged the floater wherein Sumia labored to sever her bonds and the Black Thief of Tsargol slumbered, unconscious from the blow the Princess of Patanga had dealt him. Thongor ground out a desperate curse as he saw the airboat enter the roiling mass of clouds: he well knew how easy it would be for the fleeing ship to elude his pursuit masked in impenetrable darkness. He did not know that the mysterious masked man was no longer at the controls, and that no living hand was guiding the hurtling craft.

With numb fingers and aching wrists, Sumia sawed at the bonds that constrained her. It would seem to be a simple thing to cut one's self free with a keen blade, but in actual practice it proved incredibly difficult. Bound as she was, the girl could but with infinite difficulty pass the dagger blade across the strands of rawhide that bound her wrists. She found it comparatively easy to free her ankles, holding the blade in one hand, but when it came to sawing free her hands she found it a painful, exhausting and time-consuming chore. Frustrating, too, for she had long since given up counting the number of times the heavy dagger slipped from her numb fingers and fell to the floor. At length, after what seemed like hours of slow torturous labor, she was almost free—but a single strand of tough leather remained between her and freedom—when to her horror she saw the unconscious form of Zandar Zan rouse!

She froze motionless as the Black Thief rose to his feet, passing one hand over his bloodied brow, his white face framed in an expression of puzzlement—that cleared suddenly, as he saw her with knife in hand.

With an oath, Zander Zan sprang across the cabin at her, snatching the dagger from her nerveless hands and hurling it against the further wall. Her he unceremoniously dumped on the bunk with a curt warning to be still and not to move. Then he sprang to the controls with urgent speed. How long had the floater plunged through the night out of control? How far had they come—and where were they?

Alas, the airboat's directional compass had been shattered when, struck down by Sumia's blow some time before, his unconscious form had slumped across the controls. With the compass gone, and all the air about them clouded with dark mists, the Black Thief had no means of knowing where they now were, or in which direction they were traveling!

Flying utterly blind across the unknown country, the slim craft hurtled on through the dense mists. . . .

When the craft in which his princess was held a helpless prisoner plunged into the massive, mountainous wall of mists and vanished from even his keen sight, Thongor felt a moment of terrible despair. He well knew it would be easy for the ship, thus hidden from his view, to circle beyond him and to fly thus unobserved to its secret destination. And he knew too, with grim certainty, that for all his strength and wit, he could do nothing to prevent it.

There was simply nothing for him to do.

But the mighty barbarian had not fought his way through thrice ten thousand perils to this very hour to surrender now, to yield supinely to the mockery of Fate. Breathing a savage prayer to Father Gorm that was more than half an oath, he swung his slim little craft into the floating murk and drove straight into the cloudbank after his prey.

Almost instantly his range of vision shrank to the compass of the floater's tiny cabin. The thickly-piled clouds obscured even his hawk-keen sight, as they hid from view the star-clustered heavens far above, and the great golden moon of Lemuria. He flew on through blackness as through a sea of ink.

At this height, he could not even see the land below. Indeed, did he not recall having studied what few crude maps there were of this territory, he could not have told what manner of terrain lay beneath his speeding little craft. For aught that his unaided vision told him, he could be flying above hill or plain, forest of jungle, rocky wasteland, sterile desert, or even the ponderous and dragon-torn billows of Yashengzeb Chun the Southern Sea!

He flew on through the seething vapors that coiled about his slim little airboat and lashed against the glass panes like serpents of smoke . . . searching with keen eyes for the faintest glimpse of the floater whose pursuit had carried him so far from great Patanga . . . searching with fierce, hawk-golden eyes whose indomitable gaze sought in vain for the slightest clue to the direction his agile prey had taken. . . .

Sumia huddled on the bunk while Zander Zan wrestled with the controls. She watched as the slim young man bent his black-clad body forward, staring through the murk. The thief cursed savagely this unending mass of clouds into which his floater had plunged, for he had lost all sense of direction and knew not where every passing moment carried them. Too, the Thief of Tsargol did not know what had become of the Patangan boat which had with such tenacity pursued them all this distance from the hour in which he had carried off the princess from her walled city of golden stone. For all he knew, every instant of flight carried them closer and closer to the warrior pursuing them, and farther and farther away from the safety and haven of seacoast Tsargol. In this darkness—how could he tell?

When she had seen the unconscious black-clad form awake, the princess had frozen, helpless with shock and dread. Now, however, her wits returned . . . and gradually she realized that, almost free from her bonds, she had a good chance to strike down her abductor again and even to drive the airboat back to the safety of her realm and the stronger shelter of Thongor's arms. She resolved at least to try, for nothing was to be gained by inaction—even death were preferable to captivity—and she knew that the man in black did not seek her life, else he could have slain her at any time during the length of this strange and perilous voyage.

Something caught her eye, across the narrow cabin. The icy glitter of naked steel. . . .

The dagger!

It lay against the further wall where Zandar Zan had flung it when he wrested it from her hands but moments before.

Doubt coiled in her young heart. Could she reach the blade before the black-clad thief could sense her motion, and turn to battle her? Her small jaw set with firm determination. She must try! Even though a strand of leather still bound her wrists helplessly together, she must pick up the dagger and drive it between those black-garbed shoulders, or this nightmare of captivity might never end.

Silent as a wraith, Sumia rose from the bunk beside the cabin wall and stood motionless, searching the thief's back with her frightened eyes. He was still busied about the controls and if he was aware that she had risen, he gave no indication. She began to inch her way across the cabin. It was very narrow, only a few yards, but under the desperate tension of this suspenseful moment, the distance seemed endless. Now was she glad that she had cut her legs free earlier, for had they still been tightly bound, she could never have dreamed of traversing the cabin with any stealth or silence.

Now she stooped and snatched the dagger up, rising again to her feet—and in that instant, Fate again threw his dark hand to the wheel of fortune. A vagrant gust of wind rocked the airboat ever so little, but enough to cause Sumia to fall heavily against the cabin wall. And as she fell, she gave voice to a little involuntary cry——

At her cry, Zandar Zan whirled and spied, in one swift glance, the dagger held in one bound hand. His white face, tense with the strain, contorted in a terrible grimace of icy rage. Giving a savage cry of inarticulate rage, he sprang at her like some black vandar of the jungles.

They fought there in the swaying cabin. Sumia, with a strength born of utter desperation, writhed and twisted like a striking serpent, kicking out with agile feet, striking at Zandar's face with the dagger. The slim blade flew in a glittering arc and caught him across the upper arm, slashing through his dead-black garment and laying bare his bronzed flesh which now ran scarlet from the razor-keen steel.

Mouthing an oath, he caught her arms in his slim but powerful hands and sought to wrench the dagger from her grasp.

As they struggled together, their backs turned from the cabin's forward windows, neither saw the dreadful sight that loomed up before them.

So swiftly had the airboat flashed through the sky that already it soared high above the unknown mountains of Ardath. Now the terrific winds that roared like howling demons through the needle-sharp mountain peaks rose in a furious gust of icy wind and tore away the clouds that enwrapped the floater. Suddenly, clear night skies flashed into view, and a vista of dense jungles, cloven rocks and soaring cliffs, and beyond these, to the unknown east, the trackless plains of the legended Blue Nomads. But it is of none of these I speak; none of these would have struck cold with dread the hearts of Zandar Zan and Sumia, had they glimpsed it.

It was that which lay dead ahead of them.

Straight from the low foothills of the Ardath range rose a terrible thing. A mountain lifted into the starry sky its fantastic crown of pinnacles. A mountain of black marble, vast, dark and terrible. . . .

The Mountain of Doom!

Tallest of all the mountains of antique Lemuria, the black mountain rose into the night sky like a wall of darkness. A wall of cold marble that rose a solid mile above the earth.

And directly towards it the airboat hurtled, completely out of control. Within the small, cramped cabin, Sumia and Zandar Zan fought furiously, both unaware of the dreadful wall of stone towards which their craft hurtled. Lithe as a tigress, the girl fought to retain possession of the dagger; struggled to drive it into the unshielded breast of her cruel abductor. With his superior male strength, Zandar Zan fought to tear the blade from the girl's clenched hands. Neither was able to give a moment's thought to that which lay before them.

As they struggled, the airboat flashed on, like a flake of iron drawn with irresistible force into the deadly embrace of some tremendous magnet, or a floating chip of wood pulled into the seething maw of the whirlpool. On and on the craft drove, hurtling helplessly toward the black mountain that loomed up before it like some angry giant.

Within just moments now, unless diverted from its path, the slim craft would collide at deadly speed with the marble mountain. Within the cabin the two wrestled desperately, oblivious to the danger which approached them with flashing speed, as the floater flew on . . .

. . . And with a thundercrack, shattered against the stone cliff.

Thongor never knew how much time flew past as he searched the clouded sky for some glimpse or trace of the other airboat. It seemed like measureless hours through which he was condemned to search in ever-widening circles through the muffling fog, to search without catching any sight of the elusive craft. Had he been right? Had the clever abductor of the princess doubled back in the murk, hidden from his gaze? Was he alone here in the cloudy skies over unknown Nianga?

Then, suddenly, raging winds tore the curtain of mist in twain and he flew into clear night, lit by great stars and by the enormous floating lantern of the moon. A weird vista of broken rock and savage mountain peaks whipped past beneath his keel. One great black mountain lifted ahead of him, and with a surge of terror that sent icy tendrils along his limbs, the giant Valkarthan saw the errant ship that had eluded him in the fog. Even as he watched with helpless hands clenched, it drove against the face of the cliff with a terrific shock that smashed the air boat to a shattered wreck!

Even at his distance, the impact was frightening. Metal plates crumpled like paper. Flashing fragments of torn urlium went sparkling through the air like sparks. The sound was like that of a thousand steel swords ringing at all once against a thousand shields.

A single moment before the ship struck, Thongor glimpsed a body hurl from the cabin and plunge into the abyss of darkness far below. So swift had it fallen that the warrior was not able to discern whether it was that of a man or a woman. The other, which ever it was, had remained in the airboat and must have been slain, surely, in that terrific collision. Flesh could not have withstood the furious shock!

His hand wrenched the control lever viciously, sending his speeding craft skidding about in a sharp half-circle. He arrowed toward the scene of the collision, toward the spot where the weightless wreckage of the urlium ship clung against the sheer wall of the black marble cliff. And as he flew, his heart was torn with one agonizing thought:

Only one form had fallen from the floater.

Only one person might have survived the wreck.

But which was it? The woman he loved, or the thief who had abducted her?

That terrible question remained, and would long remain—unanswered!

Chapter 5

THE BRINK OF TERROR

The grim black mountain lifted high
Its cloven crest of jagged stone . . .
Black peaks that clawed against the sky
. . . The gateway to a land unknown.
—*Thongor's Saga*, Stave XV.

Thongor's floater drifted down towards the mangled wreckage of the craft in which Zandar Zan had carried off the Princess Sumia. The crumpled wreck clung to the sheer wall of the black cliff in defiance to the force of gravity, for, even though shattered to ruin, the urlium plates whereof the craft had been constructed still retained their eerie power to resist the gravitational attraction of the Earth.

Rotors slowing, his airboat coasted to a halt beside the shattered hulk. Thongor locked the controls and went out on the small deck of his ship, which swayed buoyantly under his tread.

The moon was clear of the clouds now, and, although the golden illumination it shed was brilliant, so mangled and compressed was the wreckage of the other craft that Thongor's gaze could not penetrate the ruin to see if the corpse of one of its passengers was still within. He resolved to gain entry into Zandar Zan's ship and examine what evidence might have survived the disastrous collision at first hand. First, unwinding the anchor line from the rear of his deck, he secured his craft by tethering it to an outcropping of the cliff some yards above the deck. Testing the rope, he made certain the light collapsible grapnel-hook was tightly wedged into a broken cranny between two boulders, for should the ship drift away in the up-gusts that whistled around the Black Mountain, he would be hopelessly marooned in an unknown land far from home.

All secure, the giant barbarian cleared the low deck-rail and boarded the other craft carefully. The shock of its impact with the mountain wall had crushed its needle prow flat, splitting the urlium hull open along the seams, until the forward end of the floater resembled some mad, sur-realistic steel rose with spread petals. It was these open leaves of metal that held what was left of the wrecked floater against the cliff: tightly wedged and folded into irregularities of the sheer rock wall, they held the broken craft against it as an insect crushed by a giant's hand adheres to the wall.

The ship was almost totally demolished. About its crushed hull, a cloud of loose urlium plates and fittings floated weirdly, and the entire scene—the wild vista of this savage, barren and mountainous land, from which the mammoth black marble pylon of the Mountain of Doom rose like some colossal structure in a ruined city raised by Titans, all lit by the clear gold light of the summer moon—was like some fantastic dreamscape from a fevered vision.

Thongor carefully clambered into the wreck. The cabin was collapsed in upon itself and the rear deck was bent up almost at right angles to its usual position until it thrust perpendicularly into the air, making entry into the cabin impossible from the rear of the ship. With skill learned during his savage boyhood among the wild clans of the frozen north of the Lemurian continent, the swordsman climbed over the roof of the cabin to see if he could enter the craft from the front.

It was hazardous in the extreme. The pressure of the bent plates was all that held the wrecked airboat against the cliff, and Thongor's massive weight caused the wreck to wobble insecurely, threatening at any moment to dislodge the wreck entirely, hurling his helpless body to a terrible death in the shadowy gulfs hundreds of feet below. But the agility learned in clambering over the slick, precarious glaciers of his homeland stood him in good stead now, and he was as surefooted as a snow ape.

He found, on approaching the nose of the wreck, that a narrow ledge ran along the cliff just a few feet above the level at which the wreck lay. In the clear moonlight, the warrior judged that he might gain the easiest, safest entry into one of the crumpled cabin windows from the security of that ledge . . . so he stepped upon it.

That step was his undoing.

In reaching the ledge, he was forced to lever himself up from the shattered nose of the craft. The thrust he exerted at the focal point of the bent, twisted plates formed them loose from their tenuous connections with the cliff!

With a feeling of utter helplessness, the giant barbarian watched as the ruined ship detached itself from the cliff with a horrible, metallic screech of tortured steel and drifted clear of the wall, floating out over the gulf of empty air, leaving him behind precariously perched on a narrow ledge!

For one heart-stopping moment, Thongor thought of leaping out over the abyss of emptiness, hoping to seize hold of the weightless wreck. But almost at the same moment he decided such a move would be utterly hopeless of success. For now the ship was caught in one of the ferocious updrafts that rose out of the gulf below. It floated up swiftly beyond his reach and was gone from his view, caught in the icy gales of the upper atmosphere. Soon it was whisked from view in the mantling clouds.

Despite the cold, Thongor felt great drops of perspiration start from his brow and bare chest and arms.

Never in a life filled with a thousand perils had he stood in a more awful situation!

At first glance, his position seemed utterly hopeless. The ledge upon which he stood with his back to the wall of black wet stone was scarcely more than two or three inches wide. It ran parallel to either side of him for only a foot or two, and then the cliff fell away smooth as glass. Above his head within hand's reach there was no projection to which he might cling. As for what might lay beneath the ledge on which he stood, he had not noticed when stepping from the wreckage to this ledge, and could not ascertain, even by bending his head to the utmost degree possible.

Spread-eagled against a sheer cliff, he was suspended hundreds of feet above the earth. He could move in no direction, save to fall headlong into the shadowy abyss that beckoned beneath his booted heels. He was totally helpless. It seemed there was no means by which he might elude a brutal death on the sharp stones below. . . .

It has been said of Thongor of Valkarth that his savage heart has never known the icy touch of fear. This is not true, for what man ever drew breath, who never felt the dank breath of terror at his neck at least once in all his days? And although perhaps the mighty warrior was braver than most men, had triumphed over more enemies and escaped from more dangers than it is given to most of us to experience, in this terrible hour he knew that he had never been in a more desperate position than this.

His only mode of escape lay in his own airboat, moored some yards to his right and floating in mid-air above him. Yet the more he studied his situation, the more he was forced to realize that even this avenue to safety was hopelessly beyond his reach. Had the airboat been only a few feet nearer, he might have hazarded all on a desperate leap . . , but it was too far away. From his standing position, flat against the cliff wall with no room to set his feet, he knew with grim certainty he could never cover half the distance to the deck before falling to his doom in the shadowy depths below. . . .

There was no way out, it seemed.

Or—was there?

He suddenly noticed how the furious up-driving gusts of wind howling up from the gulfs below tossed his ship from side to side. Even as he watched, the bobbling deck rail swam several feet nearer as the ship swung slowly back and forth at the end of its anchoring line.

His face a grim, impassive bronze mask, he tensed. Great muscles coiled along his legs; taut thews swelled, gathering power in his mighty back and shoulders. His powerful arms, spread flat against the cold wet stone, crept to his sides, pressing firmly, ready to propel his body outward from the cliff in one terrific surge of strength . . . one last desperate attempt to gain the safety of his craft. . . .

And again disaster struck.

For the floater, tossed back and forth by the gusts of wind, came loose from its anchorage! The grapnel scraped ringingly along crumbling stone and fell free—and the floater was caught in an up-swirl of wind and bobbed up far above him, far beyond even the most heroic leap of which mortal flesh and blood were capable.

His position was now even more hopeless than before. If ever a man was entitled to feel black despair, it was Thongor of Valkarth, Sark of Patanga, in that bleak hour.

Perhaps (he thought) the wisest thing to do would be to let go and fall, and put an end to the torment of suspense that tore at his nerves. Cold sweat trickled down his sides, his face, blurring his vision, stinging his strange golden eyes that searched restlessly from side to side like those of some trapped jungle cat for a way out of this precarious predicament. But no . . . no. . . . With the barbarian's innate contempt for danger, and something of the civilized man's urge towards self-preservation, Thongor knew he could never voluntarily throw away his life.

He knew that, being the man he was, he would remain standing in his place for long, wearying hours until at last sheer physical exhaustion would overcome him, his legs would give way, and he would fall to his death from the side of the Mountain of Doom. . . .

Bowing his head slightly, with the wind whipping his wild mane about his brows, he silently commended his spirit to the keeping of Father Gorm, the God of his barbarian peoples.

Was it a moment or an hour later? Suddenly he came to himself. His mind had wandered and, lost amid his thoughts, the warrior had lost track of time. Only the steely nerves of his superbly trained body had served to maintain his balance on the narrow ledge. What was it that had called his attention back?

Then he saw it again.

Within the periphery of his vision, a vagrant gleam of polished metal drifted. It was the airboat!

Some freakish chance of the changeful winds had brought down his wandering craft again. Straining every nerve to keep calm from this sudden thrill of relief and hope that surged up within him, he turned his head carefully to the right.

There, only a few tantalizing yards distant, drifted the floater. In a momentary secession of the wind-currents, it drifted almost motionless—but too far to his right for him to spring upon it. So close had the wind brought it to the wall, that the forward rotors, protruding from the sides of the under-prow, scraped lightly against the sheer wall of wet black rock. Had the tiny ledge continued along the cliff to the right a few more yards, he could have inched his way along and reached the craft without hazarding a leap. . . .

If he waited, just a bit, might not the air-currents bring it closer?

Indeed, a stray gust of the updraft struck it now, lightly, and the floater edged nearer to his place, nuzzling along the wall of rock for all the world like a calf nuzzling its dam.

His muscles began to tense again, gathering strength for one last try.

The waiting was an almost intolerable strain on his already over-taut nerves. He could feel his legs begin trembling, tight thews weary from the strain of holding this unnatural position for so long.

Then, just as he was about to spring out into space, a furious gust snatched up the floater and tossed it far, far above his head. It was a heart-breaking trick of fate.

Craning back his head, he saw the ship now in perfect line for his leap . . . but twenty yards above him.

And then he saw an amazing thing!

A man clad in black, wrapped in a tattered cloak, sprang aboard the craft far above him.

Obviously, this unknown stranger had been marooned on some deeper ledge higher up the cliff. To the unknown, the mischance that had robbed Thongor of his hope had been an incredible stroke of good fortune.

Although Thongor did not know it, the black-clad man

was none other than Zandar Zan, the Thief of Tsargol. Somehow thrown clear in the moment before the stolen floater had crashed into the mountain, the Black Thief had lain in a dazed, semiconscious state on an upper ledge all this time, recovering his wits in time to realize his dangerous predicament. The chance that sent Thongor's floater drifting within his reach had been a welcome stroke of good fortune, and Zandar Zan wasted no time in climbing over the deck rail and taking control of the craft. Unlocking the controls, he set the rotors in motion, piloting the airboat away from its dangerous proximity to the Black Mountain. In so doing, he did not notice Thongor on the ledge far below, nor did he guess that this was any other than the floater in which he had voyaged so far this night, as the models were of course identical. Having been struck unconscious at the moment of collision, he did not in fact know his craft had collided with the cliff.

Although Zandar Zan did not see the Valkarthan warrior below, Thongor saw him as the airboat swung past in a sweeping curve. And black despair descended on the warrior's mighty heart. For this was the same black-clad form he had glimpsed in the window, bearing off his princess, hours and hours ago, back in far-distant Patanga.

And now Thongor knew for certain that the figure he had seen earlier—the figure that had fallen into the dark gulf from the airboat just instants before it had collided with the cliff—had in very truth been his beloved!

Surely, then, she was slain. For no woman could survive so great a fall.

With a dull mind and an aching heart, the weary Valkarthan watched as his floater swept away into the roiling mists that now cloaked the dark sky, and receded from his view.

He was alone now, and completely without hope.

The ominous creak of crumbling stone!

Thongor felt a sudden shift beneath his feet. The blood seemed to freeze within his veins. Beneath his weight, the narrow lip of stone whereon he stood was . . . *giving way!*

He held his breath, in the desperate hope that no further change was imminent. But again destiny mocked him. Again the hideous grinding sound of stone moving against stone. Again he felt a lurch, and felt his bare arms slide across the wet surface of the black stone.

Looking down, he could see pebbles spinning off between his booted feet, whirling into the black chasm below. A wisp of dust followed, and the cold wind brought to his straining ears the click of bits of stone bouncing from ledge to ledge far below him.

His jaw tightened grimly. He knew the end was very near—perhaps only a moment or two away. The narrow ledge beneath his feet would give way any second now. And there was nothing that he could do to prevent it. All his strength and courage and fighting skill were useless. He had perhaps a second or two of life . . . before he hurtled into the black deeps far below, to join the red and broken body of the woman he loved.

But Thongor would not have been Thongor, had he yielded supinely to a superior force. Through all his hard, danger-thronged career, he had many times found himself in tight straits where the only sensible thing to do was to yield.

But never before had he done so. Ever he had flung himself into the very jaws of peril, in one mad, thunderous attempt to storm Fortune in her very citadel, and snatch life from between the very fangs of death. He resolved to do so now. Rather than merely wait for the ledge to give way and hurl him into the abyss, he determined to spring from the cliff and do so of his own iron and unyielding will, however hopeless and suicidal the deed might be.

Gathering all his remaining strength, as the stone

crumbled and he tottered on the very brink of doom, he muttered Sumia's name one last time.

And then he leaped out into empty space.

Chapter 6

SHANGOTH OF THE NOMADS

> This is the song that the Nomads sing!
>   Of the lonely sky where the lizard-hawks wing,
> And the empty plains where the sighing grass
>   Bows beneath the wheels as our chariots pass!
> In a long slow thunder the caravans roll
>   To the world's far edge whereat lies our goal
> . . . O these are the lands where we rule as kings,
>   And this is the song that the Nomad sings!
> —*Caravan-Song of the Jegga Nomads*

All day Shangoth had hunted the great zulphar. He had ousted the mighty bull from the thick rushes beside the nameless river, but so swiftly had the dreaded Lemurian boar charged that the warrior had only had a chance to hurl one of the javelins he wore in a quiver over his massive shoulders. The light lance had pierced the fierce-eyed old bull in one shaggy flank, instead of ripping straight through his evil little heart. Was this a further sign of the disfavor of the Sky-Gods?

If such it were, Shangoth could only avert the black omen by slaying with his own hands the zulphar. Thus he had set after it in an easy loping stride that ate up the empty miles of the trackless plain.

The boar had struck off to the west: this much could easily be read from the bent rushes and broken earth torn beneath his trampling hooves. Later, when the plains-grass thinned out into dry-marsh tundra, it would have become more difficult to trail the brute in his furious flight. Luckily, the javelin had struck deep, and red gore splattered the tundra moss, leaving a scarlet trail that only a blind man could fail to follow. Thus Shangoth tracked the boar with ease as the hours passed slowly and the sun drifted down the vast blue dome of the cloudless sky.

You or I would not have been capable of sustaining the pace that Shangoth held to with such ease. For the warrior was no effete child of an urban culture, but one of the fearsome and almost legendary Blue Nomads of pre-historic Lemuria, a superb specimen of a stalwart race that vanished from the face of the earth many millions of years before history began. He towered eight feet high, his magnificent body nude save for trappings of dragon-leather encrusted with fantastic jewels and with precious metals. His physique was that of some fabulous gladiator of the Gods: his shoulders were broader than you or I could reach with both arms outspread, and his upper arms were larger around than the waist of a modern civilized man. Stupendous thews clothed his mighty bones, and iron strength slumbered along that woven skein of steely tendons, the sort of strength that could with ease tear a foe apart with bare hands, or cast a hunting javelin a thousand paces.

From head to heel, Shangoth of the Blue Nomads was covered with a tough blue-black hide; hairless he was, his skull as bald as an egg, his chest a swelling shield of massive bone and leathery hide. At his waist, where a mighty girdle cinched in his belly, a great war axe hung. A scimitar swung from his other hip. And clipped to the shoulder-straps of his harness was a quiver containing a dozen javelins of hollow steel. With each of these weapons, Shangoth was adept to a degree of mastery unknown to the fighting men of our day. The Nomad's life depends upon his abilities to defend himself, his family or his clan—and to do so on the instant, without hesitation or faltering. Thus each Nomad, male or female, learns the use of weapons virtually from the time he learns to walk. It is common to see children whose years can be counted upon the fingers of one hand, practicing with bladed weapons so heavy most adults of today could only wield them with difficulty.

Shangoth had held a scimitar or one of the great double-bladed war axes in his hand from babyhood. He could not remember an hour of his life when a weapon was further from him than a hand's reach. From such familiarity is bred adeptness to a degree almost unbelievable. Couple this adeptness with the all but superhuman strength of the blue-skinned giants, and you have a warrior unequalled in the most scarlet pages of human history.

Life on the great eastern plains of the Lemurian continent is one of almost constant war. War against the ferocious beasts that roam those endless plains, the gigantic dwark who wanders sometimes into the flatlands, deserting his southern jungles; or the terrible poa, the river-dragon of ancient Lemuria. From the vast sky above swoop the monstrous lizard-hawks, the batwinged pterodactyls who still survived from the Jurassic age. Among the long grasses, evil slith flowers lurk, waiting to sate their vampirous thirsts on the unwary who may chance to stray within reach of their narcotic, mind-numbing perfumes and fall prey to the fanged, blood-sucking petals of those hell-flowers. And, in the grim deserts of the south, where age-old ruins of the most ancient cities of man rear the time-gnawed stumps of shattered palaces against the cold mockery of the unaging stars, the dreadful slorgs slither in their quest for human flesh . . . the Terror of the Sands . . . the malignant and hideous woman-headed serpents wherefrom the desertlands are shunned by mortal men and lie under the eternal curse of the Nineteen Gods.

And then there is, too, that most ferocious of all beasts —man himself. For the Rmoahal are a divided people.

Each of the Blue Nomads is enemy to the other. Horde is set against horde in a state of endless war, and this state of unending conflict has lasted for uncounted millenia since the Beginning Of All Things. Were the thousand war-clans of the blue-skinned Nomads to align themselves together in friendship, a mighty empire could be built here in the flatlands of the east, among the rubble of man's first kingdoms. But war—endless, eternal, without pause or truce—is to them a way of life. Shall it ever be so among these peoples, until at last the volcanic furies that slumber as yet deep beneath the crust of Lemuria shall rise and wake and shatter the ancient land, sinking all beneath the blue sea?

Sunset found Shangoth still on the track of the wounded boar, but even the coming of darkness did not cause the young warrior to waver from his path. Shangoth was a prince of his clan. His father, Jomdath of the Jegga, was a great chief of the Nomads. Only days ago, the cunning of a scheming enemy had forced the clan elders to turn against the chief his father, driving him into exile. Exile meant death, for, surrounded by a host of natural enemies such as the great beasts who stalked these plains, what man alone and unaided could for long survive? Thus Shangoth had chosen to go into exile with his father; to stand by and permit his aged sire to enter the wilderness would have been to sentence him to death. For days now, Shangoth and Jomdath Jegga had clung to life in a rude camp amidst the plains, while a usurper ruled in the camp of their clan, back among the ruins of elder Althaar. Against this cunning foe, the prince swore undying hatred: the powerful and depraved shaman Tengri would die under his hand . . . thus he had sworn before the Sky-Gods his people worshipped.

Now the trail of dribbled blood led into the black edges of a mighty jungle. Shangoth paused to view its tremendous expanse. His people inhabited the measureless plains; wooded areas were almost unknown to them. Yet clearly the spoor of the injured zulphar led into the undergrowth, so he must follow. High into the sunset sky towered the soaring boles of enormous fern-fronded trees, the purple jannibar, the crimson lotifer, fantastic tree-tall ferns which we of today call cycads, soaring jungle giants extinct since the dim twilight of the early Pleistocene in which the Lemurian civilization flourished. Above and beyond the jungle loomed distant mountains. Beyond all, a darkly crimson sky wherein storm-clouds roiled murkily.

Shangoth paused but a moment, and plunged into the jungle. It was like stepping across some magic portal that linked two strange worlds, for with a single stride the Nomad entered the threshold of another world.

Here, all was drowned in green mystic gloom. Only a rare beam of smoldering crimson light struggled through the thick-woven canopy of boughs far above Shangoth's hairless pate. Here was a dim, weird world of silence broken only by rustling whispers . . . of impenetrable gloom wherein occasionally glowed the burning eyes of some prowling jungle thing. All was whispering shadows, strangely exciting, awesome, thrilling. Vast scaly tree trunks of darkened purple and crimson rose through the dimness like ornate columns in some stupendous cathedral. Curious blossoms blazed like clusters of gems in the vagrant sunbeams, exuding a potent blend of heady odors that heightened the similarity of the jungle scene to the incense-thick aisles of a temple. Yet still the trail of weltering gore led on down the jungle paths, and Shangoth followed.

All about him bloomed fantastic flowers. Tiralons, those weird green roses of Lemuria, nodded on the rustling breeze. The gauzy-petaled blossoms of the Dream Lotus filled the steamy air with the sleepy narcotic vapors that coiled within their gorgeous hearts. Blood-vines dangled like monster serpents from the shadowy boughs above, their hollow thorns thirsty for the touch of flesh. Sangoth did not know, but should he chance to brush against the deathly black coils they would lash about his struggling body like a tangle of living chains, thorns thrust deep in his wincing flesh, and there would he dangle helplessly while his body was drained of blood to the last scarlet drop.

Shangoth moved through the thick bushes between the scaly boles as surefooted and silent as some great jungle cat, a javelin ready in his hand, searching the jade gloom with keen eyes and sensitive nostrils. He guessed that this jungle was filled with inimical forms of life. Herein roved the fierce, gigantic vandar, the great black lions of Lemuria which often attained the length of twelve feet and were more dangerous fighters even than the sabre-toothed tigers of Central Asia. And herein, too, was the home of the terrible deodath, the dreaded dragon-cat of the jungle world, who with his three hearts and double brain was virtually unkillable. And the most horrible beast of all the millions who had walked the ancient world, the stupendous dwark that the Jungle People call "the King of Terrors." We of the modern age call him *tyrannosaurus rex*, and have but bare bones from which to conjure a picture of the giant jungle-dragon of Earth's remotest dawn . . . what then of those first men who *saw* the King of Terrors in all the titanic magnificence of his living might?

Darkness fell, and on the wings of night came a furious storm. Howling gale-winds tore and lashed the tallest trees, soaking the earth with icy rain. Lightning lit the boiling black clouds with terrific explosions of electric fire and thunder growled and boomed and muttered in the bowels of the storm. Shangoth hacked his way through the night-black jungle, his great scimitar cleaving a path for him through the interwoven underbrush. His people who roamed forever the measureless plains in their great caravans worshipped the Sky-Gods of storm and lightning, wind and rain, cloud and star and sunlight, so as he forced his way on, he chanted runes to avert the burning lances of Dyrm the Stormgod, Lord of Lightning, and the icy blasts of many-winged Aarzoth the Windlord. Yet he went forward, for the ill-omen of the boar whom his lance had failed to slay was but another sign of the enmity the Gods bore against his house. And this omen must he render null before clan-pride would permit him to return to the rough plains camp where his aged sire awaited his return from the day's hunt.

Hours passed. The storm died overhead, and the great golden moon of old Lemuria beamed down in webs of serene light. Shangoth uttered a rune of praise to the Goddess Illana, Our Lady of the Moon, and found himself suddenly at the jungle's edge where he gazed upon a fantastic scene that gripped him with primitive superstitious awe.

Before him the level mirror of a black lake stretched to the base of a stupendous mountain that loomed up against the blazing stars. The sky was clear to the east, but to the west, a mighty continent of cloud hung low over Lemuria. And from this wall of seething vapors hurtled a weird thing like a silver dragon—which flashed in the starlight like a flung spear, catching the moon's golden fire along its sleek metallic lines. It thundered against the upper breast of the mountain even as he watched with amazed eyes, and a moment or two ere it struck, he saw a fleck drop from it and fall endlessly into the still black mirror of the lake.

It seemed to be a human form, but so swiftly did it fall that even Shangoth's keen eyes could not ascertain the fact.

He left the margin of the jungle and clambered swiftly over wet stones and black sand beach to the edge of the lake, where cold black waters lapped the sloping bank of clay. Without a moment's hesitation the Nomad plunged into the death-cold waters of the mountain lake.

Swimming was an art unknown to the blue-skinned giants who wandered the endless plains in their mighty chariots. Yet the prince did not pause ere flinging himself into the depths in search of the slender form he had seen fall out of the skies. Drawing air deep into his mighty lungs, he dove into the night-black waters, and a kick of his long legs propelled him far beneath the surface.

Cold water stung against his eyeballs when he gazed about. The water was like cloudy glass, but dimly could he make out a white body drifting towards the surface. It was the body of a woman, Shangoth thought with great wonder. A woman had flown through the skies astride the bird-thing he had seen crash against the black marble mountain!

His mighty arms spread, and he hurtled through the depths of the lake towards the slowly rising body. He glimpsed nude white limbs slender and lax, and a cloudy mass of black hair. Strange was this white goddess from the night sky, of a race unknown to the annals of his folk. He swam towards her.

Surely, no mortal could survive such a fall! Surely the impact of the water, after so great a fall, must have crushed the spark of life from her soft flesh! Yet, were she indeed a goddess from the Sky-Regions where the Gods dwelt, naught of the earth could harm or mar her immortal flesh. He dove towards the floating body.

And, as he did so, another eye spied the drifting form of the Princess Sumia, Thongor's stolen mate.

In the ebon depths of the mountain lake, a weird shape uncoiled slowly, a fanged and crested head lifting atop a fluid, questing neck. Its keen senses told it that living flesh had entered the cold waters, and the thing slavered in reptilian anticipation of warm meat and hot blood. Coil after coil unfolded from the depths, as the thing began to rise towards its helpless prey.

It was a poa, one of the dreaded river-dragons of

Lemuria, and a mighty specimen of its horrible kind, nearly a hundred feet of sinuous translucent steely-muscled flesh between spined tail-tip and the fanged jaws that gaped now for the body of Thongor's mate. With a flick of glassy fins, the poa rose towards the surface, arrowing through the black water towards the dead or unconscious body of the princess.

As for Shangoth, the river-dragon sensed his rapid approach too, but no thought of danger entered its serpent-brain where hunger raged like some flaming superhuman lust. The powerful figure of the giant Nomad, dwarfed into insignificance beside the stupendous length of the monster serpent, would provide but a second morsel for the poa to savor.

Jaws stretched wide, the dragon struck.

Chapter 7

THE WAND OF POWER

Lizard's heart and brain of bat,
Dragon's blood and human fat,
Feather from a raven's wing,
Venom from a serpent's sting,
Mix it in the pitch-black night,
And call upon the Names of Might. . . .
—*Shaman's Song*

Shangoth struck! His great war axe sheared into the sinuous snaky neck of the monster poa whose fanged and gaping jaws reached for the body of the unconscious girl. In the madness of its hunger, the giant river dragon had ignored the swimming Nomad . . . but now as the keen bronze blade bit deep into its glassy, translucent hide, severing ropy muscles and clouding the dim water with a haze of gore—the poa exploded with fury!

It broke surface, tail lashing the dark waters of the lake to boiling foam. Green serpent-blood slimed down the glistening throat of the monster from the terrible wound Shangoth's axe had made. As for the Nomad, he clamped one powerful arm about Sumia and lifted her head above the black water, so that she might breathe if still a spark of life dwelt within her. Shangoth had only an instant to prepare himself before the madly blazing eyes of the poa spotted him. The snaky head lashed towards him and as the fangs came near, he dove under the surface again and, kicking himself about, swung the great bronze axe for a second blow. Water inhibited the blow from falling with full force, but still, so massive and weighty was the great bronze axe that it sank almost to the heft in the dragon's neck, just behind the shallow curve of the skull.

The thing may have died on the instant, its tiny brain crushed by the skull-shattering impact of the heavy axe wielded by all the stupendous strength of the blue-skinned giant. But life clung tenaciously to the poa, and even in death, its motor-nerves responded. One clawed foot slashed out, and struck Shangoth full in the chest. The blow smashed the air from his lungs and perhaps smote him unconscious for a few seconds. . . . The next thing he knew, he was above the waves, coughing and spitting water from nose and mouth, only his long legs sustaining him above water. His chest ached abominably, and he felt as if two or three ribs had been crushed by the dying blow from the dragon's paw. However, he still had one arm about Sumia's waist and bore the dead or unconscious girl's head above the foaming water.

Weakly, his movements hampered by the girl's body, the indomitable Nomad struggled ashore and, when he reached the stretch of black sand, collapsed with exhaustion and lay for long moments, simply resting his tortured muscles and drawing deep breaths of cool clean air into his empty lungs. The dragon, either dead or seriously crippled, sank back into the black depths of the lake, perhaps returning to his secret cave in the lake's bottom, to coil in safety and lick his wounds, or to die as he had lived, in his hidden place.

Shangoth was not seriously injured. Though his ribs ached whenever he drew a full breath into his lungs, he now decided no bones were broken, and, with the stoical endurance of his savage kind, he ignored thenceforth the pains of his beaten body. Instead, he bent his attention to the strange being whom he had rescued from the very jaws of the devil of the deep.

Shangoth had never seen a person from any race other than his own. She was obviously a woman, but in no other way did she resemble the females of his own nation than in her physical femininity. He was fascinated by the soft, tender flesh of her partially unclothed body, and by the pearly whiteness of her skin. Those of his race had hide as tough as leather, and of a blue or purple hue so deep as to verge upon black. He was also intrigued by her hair. The long wet mane of glossy black curls that poured over her shoulders and reached below the small of her slim back was something he had never seen on a human being before, as among his kind, both male and female had bald and hairless skulls. Lastly, her smallness and delicacy of figure aroused his curiosity. The women of his race were but slightly less tall than the males, and he had never seen a fully grown female less than six or seven feet tall. By comparison with the massive-limbed, powerful Nomad women of his experience, this white-skinned girl with her flowing ebon locks and slim form was elfin and delicate. He wondered from what far land she had come, and why she had ventured so far from the realm of her people. A thousand questions teemed within him. But, in all likelihood, their subject would never live to answer a one of them. For he had since given up that first notion that had flashed through him when he saw her fall from her weird flying chariot, and now felt certain that she was no goddess but a mortal woman, albeit very different from any such that he had ever seen or heard of. Surely no Sky-Goddess could be knocked unconscious, and require the actions of a lowly earth-dweller to rescue her from the fanged jaws of a poa!

She lay there against the damp black sands, deathly pale and terribly still. No warm blood flushed in her pallid cheeks. No life fluttered the thick sooty lashes that veiled her dark eyes. Her curly mane lay dank and dripping, clinging to her white body where pale limbs showed through the rents in her garment, which was by now little more than a soaked collection of tattered rags. The gold cups that clasped her breasts glittered wetly in the silver moon-rays. The strange girl that had fallen from the unknown sky worlds above had fallen to her death. No creature so slight and weak in appearance could have survived so fearsome a fall from so vast a height.

With a heavy heart, Shangoth gathered up the limp, still body in his great arms and bore it into the black jungle. The least he could do was to give it the sacred burial known to his people. He could not permit such loveliness to be torn and savaged by hungry beasts. No . . . he would find a clearing in the jungle, and there he would build a pyre of dry wood and grasses, and burn the small white body, so that its holy essence might ascend again into the unknown heavens wherein it had its home.

As he vanished into the black jungle, he did not notice that the gold breast-plates were, ever so slightly, rising and falling in slow, shallow breathing. . . . Sumia was not dead, but only unconscious. But this the Nomad did not observe as he bore her into the lightless depths of the jungle.

Jomdath Jegga stood wearily atop the low mound that stood just beyond their rude camp, wondering whether his son was alive or dead. Yesterday at dawn Shangoth had set out to hunt down the huge zulphar whose tracks they had seen the evening before at the waterhole. All the long day his son had not returned, nor through the black night wherethrough the old chief waited patiently, and now dawn had come, ushering in a new day, and still the prince had not come back to camp.

The old chief of the Jegga Nomads was tall and massive, taller even than Shangoth. His magnificent physique towered nine feet, nude save for a harness of gilded leather belts thickly encrusted with rare gems and badges of precious metals. Standing there in the gold rays of early morn, leaning on a ten-foot spear of light steel, peering out into the empty wilderness, he looked like some barbaric god. Although aged with years of kingship and war, and worn now with many cares, he was neither bent nor enfeebled. Among the blue-skinned Rmoahal, the suppleness and vigor of youth and maturity are vastly prolonged due to some genetic quirk; age, when it strikes at last, comes swiftly and wastes the body in mere days. But the lifespan of these giants who rule the vast plains is measured in centuries, and Jomdath might well look forward to many strong years of unimpaired strength before the Dark Hand reached forth to snuff out his spark of life . . . unless some foe struck him down first, he thought wryly.

Of such foes, he had many. Already had they struck, and the mighty chief tightened his grim jaw at the memory. For a hundred winters and more, he had ruled over his horde in peace and in war, and always with wisdom and justice. The long caravan of metal chariots had wandered over the endless plains of whispering grass, following the migrant herds on which they fed. They had wintered in the ruined cities of man's first kingdoms, whose broken walls and crumbling towers lifted from the trackless wastes—ancient Nemedis, the First Kingdom, that rose beside The Nameless Sea; immemorial Althaar and time-shattered Quar of the riven domes—in war-season, his people had held their own against the other clans of Rmoahal warriors that wandered the unmapped plains, drawing their chariots into a closed ring and unlimbering their mighty war-bows against shrieking hordes of enemies, who howled with war-frenzy as they assaulted the chariot-wall, their faces made hideous with red streaks of paint.

But ever a cunning and remorseless enemy plotted secretly behind his back to hurl Jomdath from his high place of power, and seize the crown for himself. This evil, scheming man was no warrior, but a sorcerer, the shaman Tengri. Rumor whispered that the shaman Tengri was secretly an agent for those dark lords of power who ruled in Zaar the City of Magicians far to the south, but as to the truth of this, Jomdath did not know.

At last the evil shaman had found a grievance he might ply against Jomdath . . . a tool wherewith he might dislodge the old chief from his seat of power. It was this: among a savage people of barbaric ways and cruel habits, a people devoted to the arts of war, Jomdath and his son the Prince Shangoth alone knew the meaning of obsolete words like "mercy" and "kindness." Indeed, Jomdath had many times spared a captive foeman the slow death of torture at the stake, granting him the merciful benison of a swift death. This had rankled with the proud warriors of the Jeğga, for, although they respected the old chief for his wise leadership in the hunt and the migrations, for his courage and ingenuity in war, and for the justice of his impartial decisions in disputes over the dividing of wealth or women, his grants of mercy to the captive foe displeased them. To them, torture was an art to be lingered over and appreciated for its subtleties. They could well remember the elder chief, Jomdath's sire, under whose hands once, a full century and a half before, a captive chieftain had lingered under a full year of torment, until death took his mangled corpse at last. They little liked the squeamish, softhearted ways of Jomdath, and the more he held them from glutting their cruelties on the helpless, the more they began to grumble against him.

The cunning shaman had seized upon this pretext to talk against the old chief. His whispers, his sly innuendos, his cunning hints and jests fanned the coals of resentment into a blazing conflagration wherein at last Jomdath of the Jegga was caught. A council of the clan elders had stripped the old chief of all rank and title, and driven him forth into the wilderness alone and unaided, to die . . . for who could survive in the wilderness alone? A thousand predators roamed the waste, against which the giant strength of a single warrior would prove feeble. Jomdath grimly knew that could the shaman Tengri have won his will, he would never have been sent forth to such a swift death as exile. The shaman would have delighted in putting Jomdath and his heir to the Death of a Thousand Knives, so that he could gloat in person over their bloody ends. But the Sacred Laws of the Sky-Gods were explicit on this point: the person of a rightful-born Clan Chief was holy and not to be touched even were he stripped of rank by the council of elders. So forth he was driven—and his son the prince joining him—from the ruined city of Althaar wherein the tribe now camped, sent alone into the wilderness to find whatever deaths the Lords of the Heavens decreed.

Thus far, they had been lucky. Only a pair of black-maned vandars had challenged them, and Jomdath Jegga and his son had battled the black lion and his savage mate to the death with their war axes. As yet, no other predator had discovered them, alone and unprotected amidst the waste. But in time. . . .

Jomdath stretched his mighty arms restlessly. His son had gone forth yesterday at this hour to seek out and slay the zulphar whose tracks they had seen near the water hole. Jomdath had no fear that the prince would not be able to best the boar in open fight, even if it proved to

70

be a fully-grown tusker. For every Nomad boy, as part of the rites of manhood through which he passes at the age of fourteen, must go forth alone into the wilderness and slay a zulphar, the totem-beast of the Jegga Nomads, whose tusks he must thereafter wear on a thong necklace about his throat, adding the tusks of every zulphar he slays thereafter in manhood to the growing chain. Status, among the Jegga Nomads, was reckoned by the number of zulphar tusks a warrior wore around his neck. And young Shangoth already wore ten such tusks, representing his kill of five of the vicious Lemurian boars. No, he had no fears from that quarter, but many beasts roam the trackless plains, and some are huger and more ferocious than the great black boar. If Shangoth had been attacked by one of the terrible lizard-hawks . . . or by one of the mighty earth-shaking dragons who tread the earth . . . of such things as this, Jomdath did indeed fear for the safety of his son.

What was that sound behind him?

Jomdath turned swiftly, but it was too late. Hard hands seized him, tearing the spear from his clutch. There were three of them, fully armed, and he had left his scimitar behind in the tent. Nevertheless, he broke their grip with a surge of his stupendous thews and lashed out with one booted foot, catching one of his assailants full in the face. He heard the satisfying crunch and snap of breaking teeth as one of his foes went tumbling back down the slope, squalling from a bloody hole that had been a mouth. Then, snatching up a tent pole, the old chief went after the other two.

They battled furiously together in the brilliant noon. He swung the heavy wood bludgeon lustily, and caught one of his two remaining opponents across the upper arm, numbing the warrior from wrist to shoulder. Sunlight flashed red fire from the other's swordblade, as it fell whirling from paralyzed fingers. Clutching his nerveless arm, the warrior fell to his knees, howling with pain.

71

Jomdath now faced but a single foeman, albeit one who held a mighty war axe in a brawny fist. He recognized the man as one of the shaman Tengri's closest henchmen. The man grinned at him, mouth working angrily, spewing oaths. Then sunlight flamed on the broad axeblade as he whirled the weapon around his head and drove it straight for the old chief.

Nimbly, Jomdah sprang backwards and let the blade whistle through thin air just in front of his burly chest, light sheening from the polished bronze.

The moment it was past, he leaped forward and drove the end of the tent pole into the pit of the Nomad's belly. Iron muscles clad the warrior's narrow waist, but the rounded end of the pole sank inches deep within his flesh, landing with a meaty *thunnkk!* Breath whooshed from the man's lungs. His rugged face contorted in a spasm of agony, paling to the lips. He folded in the middle, sagging from the nauseating impact of the blow which had all but knocked him unconscious. The axe went whirling off into the grass.

Since the other's chin was now thrust forward as he bent almost double, clutching his sore belly, Jomdath stepped forward. Stooping, he lifted a balled fist from the region of his knees. Driven by all the massed might of iron legs, heavy-thewed arms and massive shoulders, the scarred fist whistled through the air to connect on the very point of the other's chin.

The blow sounded like a butcher's wooden mallet striking a side of beef. The other was lifted several inches off the ground, and hurtled backwards, out cold.

Having thus swiftly disposed of all three of his assailants, Jomdath turned to regard the camp. And saw a fourth standing in the shadow of his tent, shrouded head to heel in a cowled black cloak, leaning on a staff of ebon polished wood at whose tip a great green jewel burned like a green coal through the shade.

"So, dog of a shaman, you were not content to let the

beasts of the wild finish me off—you came with your henchmen to do the job yourself!" he rumbled.

Naught came from the motionless figure wrapped in the black cloak but a mirthless laugh. Jomdath grimly came down the mound towards his old enemy, the bloodied tent pole gripped in one capable hand. At his approach, the other threw back his hood, revealing a terrible visage like a fleshless skull.

It was gaunt and wasted, as if scorched by terrible thirsts and hungers. The blue-black flesh had fallen away, leaving jutting bone to thrust harshly forth. From sockets like black pits of shadow eyes burned with savage mockery, and thin lips parted in a cold sardonic laugh, showing teeth long and sharp and terrible as the bared fangs of some lithe jungle cat.

The hand that clasped the rod stretched forth, and the glowing jewel at its tip brushed lightly against Jomdath's naked shoulder. Something akin to an icy, tingling blast of electric force seared through his arm, deadening it from shoulder to wrist even as his blow had paralyzed the arm of his second opponent but moments before. In the icy paralysis of the gem's touch, his fingers lost their power to clutch his weapon, and the wooden pole fell at his feet.

Again came that harsh and mirthless chuckle from the skull-like face of the man cloaked in black.

The glowing gem touched lightly across his thighs, and the old chief fell like some great beast that is brought down by a well-placed arrow. His limbs seemed to go dead as wax under the electric touch of the enchanted, fiery jewel.

Now hands gripped him from behind, forcing him up onto his knees. He regretted that he had not slain the three fallen traitors when they had lain within his power. But his ingrained traits of mercy made such acts impossible to him. Now, as swearing men trussed his hands behind him and tied his feet together, he reflected grimly that he would pay the penalty for such misplaced habits of spar-

73

ing the fallen: the fallen, it seemed, had no intention of sparing *him!*

Helpless and bound, he watched in silence as the shaman Tengri busied himself with gathering together some faggots which he ignited into a blaze with a touch of his sorcerous gem-tipped staff. Soon the fire was burning brightly.

Taking up one burning piece of kindling from amidst the fire, the shaman came over to the spot where the old chief lay securely trussed. The flames of the burning end lit his fleshless features from beneath weirdly. He was smiling his hideous perpetual smile.

"I could not leave you to the beasts, old man," he chuckled. "I am, in all things, thorough, and this matter of you and your spineless whelp of a son must be . . . *finished!*"

Grinding, he pressed the burning end of the stick against Jomdath's naked chest. The old chief grimly clamped his teeth shut, and pressed his lips together so fiercely that they went gray. He would not allow the devil-priest the satisfaction of hearing him howl, no matter how terrible the pain. The hot coals sizzled against his crisping hide. The stench of his own burning flesh was sickening in his nostrils, and although he became faint with pain, not a sound escaped him. He was dimly aware of the shaman removing the burning brand from his seared flesh, and faintly, as if from a great distance, heard him say: "There is no hurry, old man . . . we have all day . . . and I swear by the Dark Lords of Chaos, that we shall hear you sing yet!"

Dizzily, through blurring eyes, Jomdath of the Jegga saw the burning brand come near again . . . and over the roaring of his own pulse, he held to one thought through the red sea of pain that arose to engulf his dimming senses: somewhere, out there in the waste, was his son, Shangoth, who even now must be on his way back to this camp.

Through the haze of pain, Jomdath prayed to his Gods that his son would arrive in time to save him . . . or at least to avenge him. But could the prince arrive in time . . . and could he avoid being captured by the evil sorcerer himself?

The thought of his son helpless in those fleshless, claw-like hands filled him with more pain that he felt from the searing brand.

Chapter 8

THONGOR TAMES A ZAMPH

The narrow ledge of broken stone
Gave slowly under Thongor's weight
. . . Below him yawned the black abyss
And in its depths, a nameless fate.
— *Thongor's Saga*, Stave XV.

At first he fell like a stone. Wind whistled around his ears, deafening him, plucking and tearing at his cloak until it streamed like crimson wings. End over end he fell, whirling down the sky. The speed of his fall tore air from his lips and lungs. Unable to breathe, he felt his mind dimming as he hurtled downwards into the abyss of darkness that lay at the unknown base of the mountain of black marble.

Then, unaccountably, he was falling *slower*. He did not know how this could be so, but it was so, for no longer did the wind scream past his ears like raging demons, and now he could catch a breath. He gulped in the frosty air thankfully, feeling the dim shadows dispel from before his vision. He gazed about him at a mad, whirling vista of spinning cliff and wheeling sky. Vertigo seized him, and he fought against it, and in the fighting gained again some measure of control over his dizzied senses.

He was truly falling slower than before, and now he could perceive the cause of this mysterious but fortunate phenomenon.

When the narrow ledge of stone had begun to crumple beneath the Valkarthan's weight, he had not fallen, but *leaped* forth from the face of the cliff. His leap had carried him through a hovering cloud of fragments caused by the crash of Zandar Zan's stolen floater. When the airboat had cracked up against the Mountain of Doom, shards of its urlium hull-plates and fittings had been scattered, torn from the crumpled hulk of the wreck. Urlium, the synthetic isotope created by Oolim Phon ten years before, was a magic metal with the unique property of resisting gravity. It was the action of this magic substance—which "falls up" instead of down—that empowered the airboats to fly. In hurtling through a floating cloud of bits and pieces of urlium, Thongor had instinctively seized a large fragment as he fell past it. The action had been accomplished without thought, by blind impulse—with the same instinct that makes a drowning man clutch at any bit of wood within his reach.

The piece that he had seized was a fragment of the wrecked floater's aft deck rail, about three feet long. Although hollow, the rail was entirely composed of the enchanted, gravity-defying metal, and thus sustained at least a portion of his massive weight. The fragment was not large enough to entirely counteract his downward plunge, but it was sufficient to slow his fall somewhat, giving him a greater chance of surviving the terrible plunge . . . although Thongor knew with a grim certainty that if a rocky plain lay at the mountain's base, the impact of his fall would kill him, shatter his bones, or snap his spine, urlium or no urlium.

With a vast feeling of relief, then, he glimpsed a few moments later that inky surface of the cold lake that lay at the foot of the Black Mountain. As he neared the surface of the ebony mirror, he released the deck rail and dove into the icy waters, rising again to the surface shortly, where he rested, treading water, flinging back his long mane of wet hair from his eyes, peering around him.

Dawn had come at last. The long night, more filled with events than any he could remember in years, had passed. Red morning lit the smoky eastern sky and painted broad strokes of furious gold across the dark sky wherein a last few faint stars guttered feebly, like flickering candles nearly burnt out.

He was hungry and weary from the long night's strain and exertions, but he did not dare pause to rest or refresh himself. Sumia, if indeed she still lived, might be very near at this moment, and in desperate need of him.

He dove deep under the surface of the black lake and searched the dark waters for some trace or sign of her, while above the sky flamed with gold morning. When he could search the depths no more, he rose again to the surface for one final time. His powerful arms clove the chilly waves, and shortly he emerged from the lake on the shore of black sand. The shore and the outskirts of the jungle he searched untiringly for some time while day spread her bright blue banners over Lemuria. But although he virtually combed the black sand and searched the nearer portions of the jungle exhaustively, he found no slightest trace of his lost princess. The clay-like sand was too dense to reveal footprints, and the thick underbrush of the jungle's margin concealed no sign that she had come this way.

He did, however, come upon a fat, gazelle-like phondle drinking from the water's edge. This he slew and skinned and ate, devouring the juicy meat raw, as he was unwilling to spare the time to make a fire and cook the steak, although eat he must to retain his strength unimpaired.

It would seem, then, that Sumia had vanished. To this realization he was uncomfortably forced, failing to find aught that denoted her presence. At any rate, the absence of evidence permitted him to hope that in some manner she had managed to survive that terrible fall into the dark lake, even as he had. Through a miraculous accident or trick of fate, he had come unscathed from what had seemed almost certain death. Tiandra, the Goddess of Fortune, had surely been with him that hour, but he knew grimly that he could not count on luck alone: his continued safety depended on his own resourcefulness. As for his princess . . . he could only hope the Gods had smiled on her as they had on him.

He set out, as it chanced, from the opposite shore from the side whereon Shangoth the Nomad had borne the unconscious princess into the jungle, thinking her dead. He set out at a long steady lope, heading south and east, in the same direction his stolen floater had flown when he had seen it last. There seemed nothing else to do.

He ran at an easy pace under the burning noon, with a comfortable stride that ate up the miles without undue effort. He skirted the jungle's edge and struck out across a grassy, swampy area.

Although he was bone-weary, he kept up the steady, space-eating stride. Sumia stood in very great peril and loneliness, more so even than did he, lost in this unknown wilderness, if indeed she still lived, and his only chance of finding her lay in regaining his stolen airboat. So, weary and tired though he was, he continued across the marshes.

Towards the end of the first hour, he slowed and took shelter behind a mass of reeds. He had come to the first dangerous beasts he had yet encountered, a herd of mighty zamphs feeding on marsh flowers. There were six or eight of the great creatures, standing knee-deep in muddy water about a hundred paces to the west of his position. Luckily he was downwind of them and thus they did not sense his presence. From the screen of reeds,

Thongor surveyed the herd. And his strange gold eyes narrowed, as a thought struck him.

The zamph is a huge creature akin to Triceratops, growing to a length of fifteen or twenty feet and attaining a weight upwards of several tons. Their hide is thick, leathery, impenetrable and tough as armor, and a dull blue in color, lightening to a muddy yellow under throat and belly. With its immense bulk and weight, standing on four short, stumpy, rhinocerous-like legs, it would seem to be a dull, stolid, slow-moving creature. But actually the reverse is true. A zamph can break into a charge of breath-taking speed, and the tremendous strength and stamina of the monster give it limitless power. It can run without tiring literally for days on end. Among the city-building peoples of the west, zamphs are captured and tamed as beasts of burden, as later races used the ox. And Thongor knew a method by which the zamph could be used as a steed—although, from choice, he would have preferred the slimmer, leaner, swifter racing reptile, the kroter.

Thus, Thongor resolved to capture and break a zamph.

It would not be either an easy or a risk-free project, and thus the warrior devoted some thought to the problems involved. The zamph is not a meat-eater, but it is an indomitable fighter and will attack anything that disturbs it seriously. Its heavy leathern hide affords the beast maximum protection, and nature gave it a superb supply of weapons in the frontal region: a beaked, horny snout armed with a vicious horn that rises from between its small pig-like eyes, plus a huge natural shield of horny bone that rises from behind its small, tender ears to cover the thick neck with a bony protuberance that is for all the world like a natural saddle.

Thongor scrutinized the small herd thoughtfully, and selected a young bull as his first choice. It was at the height of its strength and speed and endurance, a superb bull weighing about three tons, browsing sleepily from the water-flowers. The odd contradiction of so huge and frightening a monster docilely feeding on water-lilies might have roused Thongor's amusement in another time of less urgency. He resolved on this young bull as his future steed.

The first problem was that in some way Thongor must detach this beast from the herd. He might be able to cope with a single zamph, but he had no chance of dealing with eight enraged specimens at one time.

Then, once he had separated it from the others, he must somehow render it helpless. This was no easy task. How do you imprison something that weighs three tons, and can run like an express train?

Finally, having rendered it helpless, he must devise some manner of controlling the beast so that he could make it take him wherever he wished. How do you render a wild, untamed monster like this subservient to your wishes?

Each of the three problems involved in his task was highly difficult. And not one of them but was somewhat dangerous. Yet Thongor was about to venture into the great plains, and to cross them with any sort of speed, he must have a mount. Thus, with the grim practicality of the barbarian, he set about solving each of the problems in turn. It was mid-morning before he was finished with his preparations. . . .

The zamph and his fellows had left the marsh and were now grazing sleepily on the tundra, rooting for a form of edible ground-root that grew just below the tough wiry grass. Here and there about this corner of the plain, clumps of some unnamed ancestor of the bamboo soared, some of them attaining the height of twenty or twenty-five feet. In the shadow of these bamboo clumps, several bulls and one of the older cows lay dozing. But the young bull was still hungry, and he rooted eagerly among the marsh grass.

A few feet away from where he stood champing, he spied a large and particularly succulent root lying atop the grass. He ambled over to it and snapped it up, and as he did so his weak little pig-eyes spotted another delectable specimen lying some yards further along in the same direction. He lumbered from one on to the next, rejoicing in his good fortune. These fat roots were particularly delicious, and usually he could not find them except by digging his beak-like snout into the tough net of grassroots along the surface of the plain, and tearing the upper layers of the ground up. But these delicious ones were just lying on top of the grasses, as if laid out for him!

He did not realize how far the trail of appetizing roots had led him from the herd, until suddenly—without warning—the ground gave way beneath his feet and he fell squealing furiously into a narrow, shallow pit. Unable to extricate himself, he snorted furiously and then gave voice to a full-throated roar. As he did so, something crashed down on top of him. It was a frame of thick bamboo staves, tightly lashed together with leather thongs. The frame was about twenty feet long and a little wider than the pit itself, and the unfortunate young zamph found that three crossbars wedged his head between them, one passing in front of his snout, two others wedged against either side of his bony head. As he was struggling furiously against these, a fourth bar was slammed into place behind him by some unseen hand. It slid along grooves, until wedged tightly behind and underneath his horny neck-saddle. The result was that, struggle as he would, his head was fixed immobile.

His roar had aroused the rest of the herd, some distance away. The bulls were snorting and lumbering about, lifting their beaked snouts to snuff the air for scent of some enemy. The cows were squealing in rage and terror. Now two of the bulls caught the scent of their strayed and trapped cousin, and were lumbering in the direction of the

81

pit wherein he struggled, shaking the very earth beneath their tread.

Suddenly they stopped short. A line of marsh-grass that stood between them and the pit burst into flame! At the smell of the acrid smoke, they burst and ran back in terror. Like all beasts, they feared no enemy with the same fear they felt for fire! Assembling the herd together, they swiftly made off to the north and were gone from view in minutes. The line of burning grass flamed smokily until it reached the edge of the water, where wet mud snuffed it out.

Covered with grime from head to toe, Thongor emerged from his hiding place amidst the tall reeds and complacently surveyed his captive. The young zamph had discovered that, struggle however furiously he might, he could not extricate himself from the pit that had been tailored precisely to his proportions. The soft muddy floor and walls of the pit were chewed into pulpy mush by his churning feet, but in vain, for he could find no purchase wherewith to scramble out of the pit. The corners of the bamboo frame were tied loosely with slack to four bamboo poles deep-sunk into the earth at the four corners of the pit. Pull, push, lift—whatever he did, the enraged bull could neither get his head free of the frame, nor get the frame free of his head. He subsided, wheezing and snorting dispiritedly.

Thongor had dug the pit with his broadsword, in lieu of any handier tool, although he hated dirtying his beloved weapon with such menial labor. The earth about the swamp was mushy with moisture, which made the task of digging so deep a pit comparatively easy. If the ground had been hard-packed and dry, or threaded through with tree-roots, the task would have been enormously more difficult. It had been easy, too, to cut and trim the tough but hollow bamboo stalks with his keen sword, but to lash them together into a stout frame he had been forced to unbuckle a portion of the leathern harness that clad his upper body, slicing the belts into thin thongs with the small, razor-keen dirk that hung at his girdle.

Thus far he had managed to solve problems one and two without time-consuming difficulty. The bull was captive and immobilized. Now for the third and last phase of his project.

Thongor had unclipped three steel rings from a portion of his harness. Now, heating the tip of his keen dirk in the fire he had kindled in a pit of earth and wherefrom he had set the marsh grass afire earlier, he nipped small holes in each of the zamph's small tender ears, and in his underlip.

The bull squealed lustily with rage and pain, but subsided after a bit. Barbarian though he was, Thongor did not like to cause the beast undue pain, but his need was great. The point of the dirk was heated and thus cauterized the small, inconsequential wounds. Then, kneeling on the bamboo frame that held the zamph helpless, Thongor fastened the steel rings into each ear and into the lower lip. Long reins composed of leather thongs were attached to these rings wherewith the giant Valkarthan hoped to control the beast, himself seated astride its great bony saddle just behind the head.

Thus far, all had gone smoothly.

Now came the really difficult and dangerous part.

His sword cleaned of mud and replaced in its scabbard, Thongor unfastened the sliding bamboo bar that pinned the monster's neck into the frame, and cast it away. Then, swiftly, he cut the master thongs that held the frame lashed together, and tugged lightly on one rein.

The beast exploded into a frenzy and heaved mightily, shattering the loosened frame into flying fragments. Suddenly free, the zamph burst up out of the pit—and as he did so, Thongor, standing beside it, vaulted lightly onto his back and slid down into the hollow saddle of horn. Astounded at the strange feeling of bearing a rider, the beast tore off to the south in a bellowing charge, eager to be away from this place of ominous caving-ins and obnoxious bamboo traps. He ran and ran with a clumping, bone-jarring stride, but Thongor swung freely in the saddle, his legs clamped around the zamph's neck, keeping his place without difficulty.

After awhile, the zamph's dim wits perceived the weight was still there, and slowed. Now he began to swing his massive barrel of a head from side to side, hoping to dislodge his unwanted passenger in this fashion. Thongor soon discouraged him from this sort of activity by tensing the reins slightly so that with each swing of the head, the reins pulled on the rings set in his ears. That hurt, since the ears and lip of the zamph were the only unarmored portions of his anatomy, and thus vulnerable to pain. The beast's tiny brain at last made the connection between head-swing and uncomfortable twinge of ear, and learned that when he did *not* swing his head, his ear did not hurt. And he stopped trying to dislodge Thongor in this fashion, too. He simply stood panting, head down, exhausted with rage and frenzy, and in a receptive mood for further lessons.

Now, the direction in which the floater had been flying the last time Thongor had seen it had been to the south and east. That was, therefore, the direction in which Thongor now wanted to travel. So he tugged, lightly, on the right rein. To avoid the painful tugging at his right ear, the zamph swung his huge head to the right. Thongor pulled it around further, and reluctantly, the beast turned his body in that direction. Then the barbarian tugged on the rein that was clipped to the sensitive front of the zamph's lip. The only way the beast could alleviate this discomfort was to trot forward, and so he did, finding that when he began moving forward the uncomfortable tugging at his lip stopped. He also shortly discovered, that when *he* stopped, the painful forward-tugging started again.

Before the hour was out, the beast had learned the few simple lessons that were needed to make him a subservient mount, and Thongor was satisfied. Allowing the beast to graze freely for a time and to drink from a pond, Thongor munched on phondle-meat, confident that the zamph would serve as an excellent mount. If not exactly tame or friendly, he had at least learned how to obey the few commands necessary, to stop or start, to run to left or to right.

Thus Thongor swung his curious steed towards east and south and urged him into a steady trot that was about three times as fast as a man could walk. And he rode swiftly into the vast central plain and soon dwindled in the distance, following the way the floater had gone, and was soon lost to sight under the immense blue sky of noon where a great golden sun burned fiercely and few clouds floated.

Chapter 9

JUNGLE TERROR

Beware the jungle, where dark things creep
And hot eyes peer from the shadows deep,
Where vandars stalk and serpents glide
And a thousand terrors slink and hide . . .
—*The Scarlet Edda*

Sumia woke slowly as if from a deep, refreshing sleep. She did not know where she was, and at first only her dark lovely eyes moved her pale face, roaming the dark jungle clearing. She did not know how she had come to be in this place . . . the last thing she could recall was . . . was. . . .

Sat sat up suddenly, remembering the Black Thief, their desperate struggle for the knife there in the swaying cabin of the hurtling floater, and the terrible black cliff swinging towards them, glimpsed over Zandar Zan's shoulder through the forward windows!

She remembered tearing from his clutches—plunging from the cabin onto the wind-whipped deck—and then the giddy spell of vertigo that seized her and tumbled her over the rail ... falling ... falling. ...

Somehow she had been miraculously preserved from a terrible death. But how had she survived the fall? And where in the Name of the Nineteen Gods was she?

The sudden motion of sitting up awoke a thousand twinges of fierce pain that lanced through sore and aching muscles. Although Sumia could not know it, the simple laws of physics had saved her. A falling body doubles and triples its velocity and, in a very short time, is falling at such speed that breathing becomes impossible: the air whipped past Sumia's lips and nostrils so swiftly that she could take none of it into her lungs, and soon blacked out from oxygen-starvation. She had thus been completely unconscious and limp when she struck the water, and this had saved her from the broken bones or shattered spine that would probably have resulted if she had been conscious when she hit the water, as she would have instinctively tensed. But a limp and unresistant body has less chance of taking injury than one tense. Add to this the fact that Sumia had struck the water feet-first, which is the safest way, and by, sheer luck, at exactly the perfect angle to give her maximum safety. Her long legs had sliced into the waves and she had gone under without any injury, whereas had she struck at the wrong angle, or struck flatly, she would probably be dead by now. As it was, though, she ached abominably in every muscle and tendon, and her flesh was one great bruise. She felt as if she had been beaten all over from head to foot. She did not mind this, however, knowing that she was lucky to still be alive, and being a healthy girl in superb physical condition, it was not long before her groaning limbs became supple and easy again.

But how had she come into this jungle clearing? As she

gazed about, she realized that there could only be one explanation for it: someone had carried her here.

WHO?

She examined herself, finding her arms and legs were unbound, her clothing damp. Then experimentally she strove to stand, and, after several attempts, managed to struggle to her feet. Leaning against a tree, she peered about. There across the clearing was a curious pile of dry wood and leafy boughs arranged something like a funeral pyre. She wondered what it all meant. . . .

Then she froze immobile in stark horror.

A giant figure had entered the clearing, bearing an armful of dry fern-boughs. It was a figure of nightmarish horror; she could dimly make it out by the crimson glow of sunrise that permeated the leafage above. An eight-foot-tall giant of a manlike thing, naked save for a jeweled harness, and, although manlike in form, totally unlike any human being she had ever seen before, with his hairless blue-black hide and stupendous muscular development. It took Sumia but an instant to realize she had somehow fallen into the hands of one of the dreaded Blue Nomads, the Rmoahal warriors of the mighty eastern plains.

She watched, frozen, as the weird giant placed his armload atop the pile. Was this pyre for—her? She knew the Rmoahal were barbaric savages devoted to warfare—were they man-eating cannibals as well?

Leaning against a nearby hummock of turf was a quiver filled with slim, barbed javelins. Sumia stole a glance at it —then looked swiftly back to the blue-skinned giant. His back was still turned to her. He had not looked at her since re-entering the clearing. Carefully, cautiously, she stole a few feet into the open space, and, bending stiffly, slid two javelins from the Nomad's quiver.

Just as she did so, the Rmoahal rose and stiffened, searching the air with geen ears. Had he heard the scarcely-audible *clink* the steel javelins had made as she withdrew them from the dragon-hide quiver? In an instant he would turn to see her——

Without thought, she raised the slim spear in one hand and tensed to sink it through his broad back.

A growl of thunder behind them both!

She whirled, to see the great hideous snarling visage of a gigantic bristling black boar peering through the dank underbrush. She caught a glimpse of mad red eyes burning like coals, of bared yellow fangs beslavered with dripping foam—and then the huge bull zulphar shot from the foliage straight for her throat like a shaggy black thunderbolt of vicious rage.

Had Sumia been some pampered child, she might have frozen immobile with sheer panic, and thus have fallen beneath those clashing tusks and slashing hooves. But the women of her people were accustomed to the hardy life of seige and camp and field, were expert in the use of arms, and as often as not, fought side by side with their men amidst the carnage and slaughter of the battlefield.

Thus, Sumia acted without thought or hesitation—she cast the slim javelin with one smooth, fluid motion of rippling strength. The dart flashed with a bright glitter of polished steel—and quenched its brightness in the shaggy throat of the monster boar. With a coughing grunt, the burly zulphar crashed to the mossy turf, its spring botched by the striking spear. It rolled over, and sluggishly made as if to rise. Reeking gore splattered its bristly fur, splattering the dry grass with clotted crimson. But before the wounded beast could gather its legs beneath it, to propel it again at the girl's white throat, Sumia struck a second time. The second javelin flashed in the firelight and shot directly between the wide, foam-lathered jaws which snapped futilely together upon the metal shaft—then opened slowly, to belch forth a great foul-smelling rush of thick blood. The zulphar sagged back against the grasses, twitched once or twice, and lay stiff, eyes glazed and filming.

There was a long silence, as tension drained from the two. Then the Nomad turned to the girl, and saluted her by touching his heart after the custom of the Jegga clans.

"I had thought you dead," he said simply. "But behold, you live! I had thought to free your spirit in the flames, so that it might ascend again unto the Sky-Gods who fashioned it in the Beginning Of Things, but lo! it is you who do me a great service. For a day and a night I have sought to track that bull zulphar that I might slay him and remove the Curse of Heaven from my endeavors . . . but it was the bull who would have set my spirit free, had not you struck so swiftly and so surely. Now in all of this do I see the Will of Heaven exemplified . . . you, whom I saw fall from the shining steel bird into the dark lake, you who came down out of the Gods' Country, have served to fulfill my vow to the Gods. There are great matters here," he concluded, bowing to her gravely, "and thus I ask: are you a goddess? And, if you are, what would you of Shangoth of the Jegga Nomads?"

Sumia smiled faintly with relief. Now that he spoke could she see that although a barbarian, the blue-skinned giant was no blood-thirsty ogre of cruelty, but just a man, albeit a strange one of odd appearance. The girl very sensibly reflected that neither could Shangoth help his terrifying outward appearance, which seemed terrifying to her perhaps largely because his people were strange to her, any more than she could help her own appearance, which might very well seem equally as strange to him.

She said, "Nay, friend, no goddess I, but a mortal woman who is, at this moment, tired and very hungry. I am Sumia, Sarkaja of Patanga the City of Fire, and since I know that the folk of your people inhabit only the most eastern regions of Lemuria, then I know that my own lands are far to the west of this place."

He made a comfortable seat for her by partially demolishing his pyre and spreading soft grasses and leafy boughs upon a mound of earth. Then, as she relaxed wearily, glad to rest her limbs which still ached from the impact of her dive into the lake, he swiftly set about to produce a meal.

"Weariness passes only with time, Princess," he observed with a quiet smile, "but as for your hunger, we may alleviate that quickly!" And he set about skinning the dead boar and cleaning the meat. Within a very little time, succulent pork was roasting over a roaring fire, filling the clearing with an odor indescribably delicious.

While they ate they talked together, and each explained the adventures that had brought him into contact with the other. Then, exhausted by her exertions and the terrible experiences of the long night, Sumia slept while the blue giant stood guard over her with his quiver of javelins and great war axe.

After an hour or two the girl awoke from her deep, refreshing nap quite rested, and the two proceeded through the jungle together. Sumia was thankful that if her beloved Thongor could not be with her, at least she had the mighty Rmoahal warrior to accompany her, so that she did not have to face the dark terrors of the jungle alone, on foot, and without weapons.

As there was nothing that Shangoth could do to help her return half-way across the continent to Patanga, he persuaded Sumia to come with him into the plains unto the comparative safety of the camp he shared with his exiled father, the old chief Jomdath Jegga. Sumia was grateful for this offer of shelter, for she feared that Zandar Zan might very well have escaped the crash of the floater and might be searching for her. Far safer to be among friendly folk, even if they be savage barbarians, than among civilized folk who are your enemies.

Morning was high in the east when they emerged from the jungle and the girl first looked upon the trackless expanse of the great Lemurian plains. The level waste with its featureless broad monotony, over which brooded a melancholy sense of timeless desolation and mournful emptiness, filled her with a sense of grim foreboding, but no other avenue to safety presented itself to her than this, so she strode manfully along beside the blue-skinned giant as he related the tale of his father's woeful betrayal at the hands of the cunning and vengeful shaman, Tengri.

The girl had doubted whether her sore and weary legs could carry her very far; she soon discovered, in the cool freshness of the morning air and the rich brilliance of a bright sun beaming down from amidst a crisp blue sky, that the stiffness eased slowly from her limbs and, ere long, she was striding lithely beside the giant warrior without discomfort. The calm and friendly Nomad strode through the long whispering grass, talking quietly to her of his people and their ways in his deep guttural voice, the conversation helping to make the miles fly past without her notice. She found his tales fascinating, and himself curious and interesting. It was fortunate that she could understand his mode of speech, which, although curiously accented and varying from her own in several words and a few pronunciations, was still basically the same language. The human race, of course, had sprung from the hands of the Nineteen Gods too recently for the widely separated nations of Earth's first continent to have diverged as yet very far on different linguistic paths.

Sumia was fascinated by his fieldcraft. He was nearly twice her height and several times her weight, but strode so softly and lightly through the thick grasses that they barely crunched beneath his tread nor whispered to his sinuous passage. What a superb huntsman this mighty warrior must be! As tireless and enduring, as sure-footed and silent as the beasts upon which he preyed. . . .

She was curious, too, as to the mystic sixth sense by which he could find his way through the plain. Sumia would have been lost the moment she could no longer glimpse the jungle's edge or the black bulk of the Mountain of Doom which lifted behind it. But Shangoth moved in a straight line across the measureless waste, drawn towards the site of his father's camp as surely as the needle of a compass is drawn to the uttermost and ultimate north.

She was just silently observing his weird homing instinct, which, in fact, was universal among the Rmoahal of the plains, who spend their entire lives in wandering the tremendous thousand-mile wastes of the eastern coast, when she noticed a look of puzzlement upon his heavy features. Several times he halted, casting a searching look to either side of them. Once he paused for long moments, head bent as if deep in thought or perhaps consulting within himself that strange sense of direction that she found so curious. At length she was moved by this series of pauses on his part to address a question to him as to what was the matter. His reply was baffled, and he seemed disturbed.

"I find myself . . . somehow unable to be certain in which direction we are traveling," he confessed, as if it was to him a matter of shame.

They continued on for some time in the direction which Shangoth felt was the correct one, but the giant Nomad was worried. The ambiguity as to direction was a sensation new to his experience, and he found it disturbing in the extreme. It was as if some unknown force was subtly tampering with his sense of direction. He could almost feel the chill aura of some dark and nameless force reaching its eery tendrils into the web of his mind. And a feeling of ominous malignancy grew within him with every stride he took. These were dubious and unsafe regions into which his sire and himself had been forced by the shaman's enmity to take refuge. These lands in the south and east of Lemuria were under the dark mastery of Zaar the City of Magicians, that evil metropolis in the desert where the Black Magicians dwelt, who worshipped with grim rites the primal and dread Lords of Chaos who ever sought to undermine and destroy the Universe of Stars, that bright creation of the Gods of Light with whom they had warred in the shadowy ages Before The Beginning of Time. Shangoth's people never ventured this far south, and above all created beings, feared and hated the Sorcerers of Zaar.

And to the Nomad's rising fear, this supernatural meddling with his direction-sense savored of the dark wizardry of the Black City....

Now the very complexion of the land itself seemed to change, to alter strangely. Outcroppings of rock showed here and there amidst the long plains-grasses and the grass became, by stages too gradual almost to notice, sour and lank and colorless. The clear blue sky seemed grayer, overcast, for although no clouds were visible in the clean vault above, a dark web seemed to come between the Sun and them.

They breasted a shallow hill, and saw the ebon tower.

It soared up from the gray earth like a stalagmite that rises from the gaunt rocky floor of some dark cavern. It seemed natural, not man-made, even . . . *organic*, in the uneven contour and misformed shape of it. Shangoth's keen vision could not make out the jointures of the stones that composed the black spike of a building. It rose sheer and glassy-smooth, ugly and malformed somehow, as if constructed by a mad brain.

And Shangoth knew with a dire certainty that his directional sense had, indeed, been led astray by foul sorcery . . . he needed no further evidence that the sight of that hideous structure and the sense of formless terror that welled up within him at his first glance of it.

High atop the sleek and swollen height of the ebon tower, clutched in its cloven, spiky crest, a huge crystal glared down at him, filmed with green fire, blazing like some giant eye, and his hide prickled as if obscurely aware of the scrutiny of some malign and hidden intelligence. He could not tear his eyes from that glaring gem of coiling fire, even though Sumia shrank against him, and spoke to him sharply.

Against his own volition he felt his feet moving. Down the shallow slope and onto a gritty, cindery path that led to the magician's tower. Sumia cried out to him and bade him stop . . . but to no avail, his feet seemed chained to a treadmill and he must keep them moving. At last it seemed some tinge of the grim fascination reached her mind as well, for Shangoth was vaguely aware that the girl walked beside him towards the dark tower.

Like two somnambulists caught in the same hypnotic dream, the blue-skinned giant and the slender girl entered the shadow of the tower and were swallowed up within its darkness. . . .

Chapter 10

ROSE-OF-DEATH

And on across the empty plain
The great zamph bore him far,
And all the while his princess lay
In the iron hands of Zaar . . .
    —*Thongor's Saga*, Stave XVI.

Jomdath of the Jegga did not faint before the touch of searing pain, nor did he flinch from the approach of the glowing coals, such was his mastery over himself. But through the red haze that blurred his vision he knew the black hand of despair lay upon his heart. For unless his son, Shangoth, came to his aid, naught lay ahead for him save hours of unending torment and the final peace of death. For where in all these lands could he find a friend among these warring Rmoahal, whose every hand was raised against each other?

He watched the smirking shaman's face as the branch tipped with glowing coals approached his chest again—

and then he became dimly conscious of a fantastic series of incredible events to which he could assign no conceivable cause.

As the shaman reached forth the burning brand *he shrieked!* Shrieked, and stared with goggling eyes of astonishment at his right hand! Suddenly, as if by magic, a steel dagger had flashed out of nowhere, and tore through the shaman's flesh, pinning his claw-like hand to the burning branch. As Jomdath stared, he saw the dagger-pierced hand convulse with searing pain, a bloody dew glistening over it as the shaman went gray to the lips with pain—pain which he could inflict with such relish, pain which he himself could not endure. Feverishly the gasping wizard clawed at the dagger-hilt with his uninjured hand, striving to tear it from his flesh.

"Help me, you fools—the *pain!*" he babbled, writhing. His henchmen, who stood gaping in blank astonishment, awoke from their paralysis of surprise, and fumbled to assist him. Then a living juggernaut plunged into them.

Out of thin air, as it seemed, a gigantic bull zamph appeared in a thunderous rush that shook the earth. One warrior turned, sword in hand, and the bull gored him with his mighty horn—thrust him a dozen yards away—and wheeled to trample the second into a gory, battered hulk.

Just as swiftly as he had struck, the zamph stilled and stood motionlessly. A wild figure sprang from his back—a bronze-skinned swordsman, his superb physique naked save for a harness of black leather and a mighty crimson cloak that swung from his broad, bare shoulders like fantastic wings. In one brawny fist this mystery warrior clasped a great sword of blue steel that flashed terribly in the sun. He vaulted from the back of the now-quiescent beast, and hurtled towards them.

The shaman snatched up his long staff that was tipped with the green-glowing gem that had stricken down Jomdath earlier. The weird gem flashed towards Thongor of Valkarth, for of course it was he. But this time the wand of power did not strike—the Northlander's broadsword struck first, snapping the wizard's staff in twain, the magic gem falling into the dust.

With a screech of terror, the crippled Tengri flung himself aside, avoiding the arc of flashing steel, and half-ran, half-staggered towards his chariot which stood half a hundred paces away at the further edge of the old chief's camp. The last of his henchmen, the one whose arm Jomdath Jegga had broken, fled with him. Thongor looked after them, then shrugged, and bent to assist the older man, letting the villians flee as they could do no further harm.

His dagger he had left in Tengri's crippled hand, so he used the narrow point of his great sword to cut the chief's bonds. Then he gently assisted the Nomad to rise, and supported him across the field into the shade of his tent. He left him there while he went to fetch water and clean cloths, finding them within the tent. He stooped, and with a hand as gentle as a woman's he cleansed the old man's wounds, and, drawing from his belt-pouch a phial of pungent healing salve, he treated the burns and cuts and bound them carefully in clean wrappings.

All this was accomplished in mutual silence. But when he was done, Jomdath thanked him with simple dignity.

"*Belarba*, friend!" the old chief said, nodding with dignity, "I know not who you are nor from whence you come, but I thank the Sky-Gods that you were near enough and were disposed to render me succor in my time of need. I am Jomdath, once chief of the Jegga Nomads, now but a tribeless wanderer, cast forth to live or die at the mercy of Heaven. But all I have is yours—and within the tent you will find a skin of wine; I propose we share it."

Thongor acknowledged the other's thanks with a nod.

"*Belarba*, chieftain," he said, repeating the Lemurian word of greeting. "I am Thongor of Valkarth, once a tribeless wanderer from the Northlands, now a king in my city of Patanga far to the west. Happy am I that I was near enough to come to your assistance. And, as for the wine, I will go and fetch it . . . the day is hot, and I have always found that man-fighting is a thirsty business," he concluded, grinning, and vanished into the tent, reappearing a moment later with a fat phondle-skin of wine. Seating himself beside the resting chief, he drank deeply of the sour but stimulating beverage, then held the skin so that the other might refresh himself.

"Never have I seen a man such as yourself," Jomdath confessed, once he had refreshed himself to the point that the curiosity he kept in check from natural courtesy was loosed. "Are all men in your western realm such as yourself—brown of skin and slight of stature, and do they all cover their pates with that odd headdress?" he asked, indicating Thongor's savage mane of black hair which streamed down over his broad shoulders. The Valkarthan repressed a grin of amusement with some difficulty: among his own kind, of course, he was judged somewhat taller than was average . . . here in this new world of the unknown east, among these nine-foot blue-skinned giants, he had suddenly assumed the proportions of a pygmy!

For hours the great zamph had maintained a steady pace to south and east across the endless fields of dry grass. The beast seemed no longer to resent the strange feeling of bearing a rider; but, then, these creatures had small and sluggish brains, contrasting oddly with their enormous strength and iron endurance, for which reasons they were easily domesticated and used by the Lemurians as draft animals, much as the people of later aeons came to use the yak, the bull, and the elephant. Perhaps the zamph's tiny brain had become so accustomed to bearing Thongor's weight upon his shoulders, that it seemed natural!

At any rate, the young bull was obedient to the reins and carried Thongor at such a steady, distance-devouring pace, that the lulling rhythm of his stride soon caused the weary Northlander to doze there in the great horny saddle upon the monster's neck.

Thongor never knew exactly how long his slumber had lasted. He awoke with a start. Something had triggered his keen barbaric senses with alarm. Then his sensitive nostrils detected it: the scent of smoke! Tugging on the reins, he slowed the zamph to a walk, while he searched the surrounding countryside for some sign of inhabitance. He soon saw a small camp ahead.

He reconnoitered it with great caution: this was new and unknown country hereabouts, and any men might be enemies as easily as friends. Better to be sure, than sorry.

There were five men in the camp, one lying bound, being tormented by the others. Thongor knew them at a glance for Rmoahal, for he had seen the blue-skinned giants of the east before. In Thurdis, where once he had served in the legions of Phal Thurid the Mad Sark as a mercenary sword, the Rmoahal were used as slaves, although this custom was new to the cities of the west.

His lips tightened grimly. Three warriors and a fourth, some kind of priest or wizard from his robes, were torturing a bound and helpless man with a branch whose end was tipped with burning coals. Thongor's jaw tensed at the sight of this, and disgust was clearly written upon his grim impassive face. His was the barbarian's stoical acceptance of pain and death as natural conditions of life; his, too, the simple code of the savage, that demanded for an enemy a swift, unlingering death. This sick pleasure in prolonging a foe's anguish ran counter to his rude chivalry.

Then, too, the bound captive was an older man. Thongor could not help but admire the old man's majestic and unshaken dignity under his torment. Not a whimper was wrung from his firm-pressed lips. He neither raved nor begged for mercy, but endured the poignant pain with iron silence and a manly contempt for his sniggering tormentors. Thongor's blood rose hotly, one hand clenched about his sword hilt until the knuckles whitened under the pressure. At last, he could bear to watch no longer; nor could he, in honor, simply withdraw from the scene, although his quest was one of pressing urgency.

He goaded his zamph into a charge. And, drawing a dirk from his girdle, he hurled it straight and true—flashing to its mark, pinning the shaman's hand against the burning instrument of agony. . . .

They talked, acquainting each other with their adventures. And although Thongor itched to be about his search for the floater, he knew he could not simply go off and leave the old man here alone. For, should his enemies return later with augmented strength, Jomdath would be at their mercy, since he was still weak from his pain, although rest and wine had restored a measure of the old man's strength. They discussed the problem of what to do.

"Now that this hell-spawn of a shaman has tracked the old vandar to his lair, I can no longer remain in this campsite to await the return of my son, Shangoth," the old chief said.

"But can you go elsewhere?" Thongor questioned. "When your son does return from his hunt, how will he know where you have gone—since any message you might leave behind, describing your new whereabouts, might well fall into the hands of your enemy, should the shaman return to seek you again as you predict he will?"

Jomdath smiled quietly.

"We foresaw this eventuality, and ere my son left camp yester-morn, we selected an alternate campsite two miles further south of this place, by a rise of hill-land. I will leave a certain mark in the earth when we go—it will seem meaningless to any eyes but those of Shangoth, and will tell him that I have gone thither."

"Then, if you are strong enough to ride, let us go there now," Thongor urged. The old man rose, albeit a bit stiffly, and in less time than it would take me to tell of it, they struck camp and, mounted both on Thongor's steed, were ready to ride off into the trackless south. But, ere they quitted the camp, Thongor stooped and plucked from the trampled dirt the broken end of the shaman Tengri's staff whereon the weird green gem still flashed and smouldered with curious inner fires.

"The shaman swung this at me as if it were some sort of weapon," the Valkarthan observed, turning the gem curiously from side to side with gingerly fingers. A curious thrill of power tingled along his nerves from the touch of it, and he puzzled to see how it was fastened to the end of the ebony rod: a thin hole had been bored through the axis of the crystal with some strange art, and a narrow rod of iron transfixed it from pole to pole, obtruding from either faceted face as an odd nodule that a person of our own age might have recognized as somewhat akin to an electrode.

The chieftain related how the gem's touch, as wielded by the shaman, had robbed his body of all power to move. It was an odd, perhaps even a valuable, fact, and Thongor tucked this scrap of lore away into his mind, even as he thrust the small crystal, wrapped in a bit of cloth, into his girdle-pouch for later study. A gem of such magic powers might well come in handy another time, he thought. . . .

They rode south with no further delay, as the sun declined down the steep sky and the long shadows of afternoon fell across the endless plains. Here the abundant grasses fell away and the land became sere and barren. It was as if, the further they went and the nearer they came to the southernmost land wherein rose the dread black city of Zaar, the more dead and drear became the very face of the earth, as if all nature shrank back in awe and loathing of that kingdom of Black Magicians here at the earth's remotest edge.

They rode through dry gullies that perhaps had once been the bed of an ancient river long since dried to its very source, or somehow diverted from its age-old path. A curious stillness came into the air, together with a gathering tension . . . a sense of . . . *expectancy*.

Thongor did not like it. His keen barbarian senses told him that danger lurked about here, a danger that he could not see, a danger that he could only *feel* in some weird extrasensory manner. His skin roughened, as at the clammy touch of a chill, uneasy wind that moaned along the banks of dead earth. The sky was gray, now, gray and overcast as if by hovering but invisible wings . . .

What was the strange odor . . . that pungent and growing sweetness on the breeze? Never had he smelled that sickish, almost overpowering perfume.

Of course—the flowers. For now the zamph ambled sleepily through a broad, level field of odd blossoms whose like Thongor had never seen before in all his wanderings. Large, fleshy petals clustering about a heart wherefrom sprang a long glassy tube-like protuberance. The flowers were all about them now, brushing thickly against the slowly-moving flanks of the great beast whereon they rode.

The oddest thing about them was their unnatural color. Never had Thongor seen or heard of any flower with petals like these, of dull satiny *gray* . . .

Their scent rose in heavy clouds of oily vapor, cloying, super-sweet, almost overpowering in their pungency. Beneath the sense-deadening sweetness of them, lurked a musky stench that somehow revolted the Northlander's keen nostrils . . . a musty stench like a serpent's nest, an effluvlia of dead things gone rotten . . . obscurely, he thought to speed the pace of the zamph—something told him he should be gone from this unwholesome garden with great haste—but the beast would not hasten his pace.

The sense of danger clamored through his brain, like ghostly voices striving to rouse him from a perilous lethargy. He could not understand it . . . perhaps if he could close his eyes for just a moment. . . .

The old chief, behind Thongor, had been dozing, worn out from exertion and torment, and was awakened only when the heavy weight of the Valkarthan sagging in the saddle threatened to dislodge him. He nudged the almost unconscious Thongor back to wakefulness. Groggily, Thongor roused, and settled more securely in his place, mumbling something about the damnable stench of these *gray flowers. . . .*

A thrill of superstitious fear darted along the old chief's nerves. He sat bolt-upright in the saddle, and shook the slumped form of his companion desperately.

"*Gray* flowers! Thongor—wake! Ride for our lives—we have strayed into a garden of terror!"

"What . . . what are you talking . . . about . . . ?"

Again he shook the Northlander awake.

"We have strayed into the reach of that flower of hell the lore-masters call Rose-of-Death!" he shouted hoarsely. "The blooms exhude a narcotic vapor that dulls the senses of the unwary, and clouds their wits, sending them into a sleep from which they shall never awaken! *The sleep that ends in death!* For as you slumber, the flowers' tendrils will drain the red blood from your body and leave you a withered husk—ride, Thongor—ride!"

But it was too late. The Valkarthan slumped over and fell heavily from the saddle into a hillock covered with the gray hell-blossoms.

As he struck the earth and sprawled unconscious, his face buried among the gray flowers, he dislodged something that was hidden under the petals, and it rolled down the shallow little slope to the bottom . . . a gaunt, grinning skull that had been stripped bare of every atom of moist flesh and lay bare dry bone, grinning up at Jomdath Jegga as he swayed drunkenly in the saddle, and, reelingly, fell himself into the soft odorous embrace of the field of Rose-of-Death.

Fell, and fought for a few moments more, his lungs filled with a perfume overpoweringly sweet, then struggled no more and lay face downward as one dead.

The zamph stood for a while, dimly wondering if his riders would mount again soon. He ambled over to Thongor and nosed him curiously, snuffling the sickening odor . . . then fell to cropping the gray blossoms. But their flavor sickened him. He snorted and spat them out, and wandered away to seek greener grass and more wholesome sustenance. Soon he was gone from sight, wandering off to eventually rejoin his herd. The two bodies lay stricken and deathly silent amidst the field of gray blossoms.

Then something stirred about the nearer blooms. The slender transparent tube that grew from amidst their petals, twitched . . . quested about . . . brushed along Thongor's naked side. Other tendrils probed down . . . and began to—*drink.*

Chapter 11

CITY OF A THOUSAND AGES

> Strange and desolate are these mighty plains of
> the east, haunted with memories of past aeons,
> where rise like haggard ghosts of dead yester-
> day the ruined cities of the first kingdoms of
> Man . . . and there in the age-haunted, ruin-
> cumbered east lies both an old darkness and
> the bright dawn of a new day . . .
>
> —*The Great Book of Sharajsha
> the Wizard of Lemuria*

Zandar Zan was a frightened man. And a deeply worried
one, as well. Almost from the very first, his dark plans had
gone awry—through no fault or oversight of his, to be
sure, but awry nonetheless.

First, he had failed in his attempt to kidnap both Sumia
and her son, Tharth, the infant Prince of Patanga. The
sudden intervention of Thongor had shattered that plan
to atoms, and had forced the Black Thief to flee with only
the princess for prize. His masters in seagirt Tsargol
would not be too deeply pleased with that failure, even
though failure it was in part only. But that was only the
beginning of Zandar Zan's troubles.

Almost from the first moment of his flight from Patanga
the City of the Flame, had he been closely pursued by another fleet airboat. This, too, was not according to the
plans of the Thief of Tsargol, and it had made it impossible for him to fly directly to the city of his masters.
Instead, he had been forced to take another, wider route
into the east where he had hoped, under cover of the dark
night and masking his actions behind a mighty veil of

storm-clouds, to shake off the speeding airboat that clung to his tail, hotly pursuing him in his every attempt to shake it off and lose it among the clouds.

For ten hours he had hurtled east and ever east, while his superb craft ate up the flashing miles. Then had come that frightful accident—the unexpected collision with the Black Mountain that soared up from the Ardath range—and his prize, the Sarkaja Sumia, had been flung to a hideous death in the gloom-veiled chasms far below, while he himself had sprung clear to a rocky ledge where he had lain stunned, bruised and shaken, lost halfway across the mighty continent of Lemuria, hopelessly marooned atop the tallest mountain of the world.

Only the fortuitous whim of destiny had flung a chance for life his way, when the pursuing airboat had come within his reach and he had been able to clamber stiffly aboard. At first, dazed and not fully realizing what had happened, he had mistaken this airboat for the one in which he had fled hither from the city of Patanga. But, ere long, he discovered his error through the simple fact that this craft possessed an unbroken directional-sphere, whereas the one in his ship had been smashed through the actions of the captive princess.

He had, then, taken the floater of his unknown foe—who had tracked him relentlessly across half the breadth of Lemuria, only to fall prey to some mysterious fate on the mountainous cliff. Zandar Zan did not know that it had been Thongor, the mate of the girl he had carried off, who had piloted this floater in hot pursuit of his stolen mate . . . nor did the Black Thief guess that by seizing the unmanned airboat, he had changed places with the great Sark of Patanga, leaving him marooned on the black marble cliff even as Zandar Zan had been. Nor did he know, of course, that by a slender margin—or a miracle—Sumia had survived the fall into the dark chasm beneath the Mountain of Doom.

He only knew that he had failed—*disastrously.*

He no longer had Sumia a captive; he had never managed to seize the infant Prince of Patanga—now, if and when he returned to Tsargol to confront Yelim Pelorvis the High Priest of Slidith Lord of Blood, and Numadak Quelm who represented the broken and outlawed cult of Yamath the Fire-God, and the others who had plotted to lure Thongor into destruction and to conquer his young empire—he could not give into their hands the living prize that would lead to the whelming of Patanga!

From this failure, he grimly knew, there was no way out. The Thief of Tsargol, whose keen wits and agile skill had served to extricate him from a thousand traps and perils, was trapped now, once and for all. There was nothing that he could do that would in any way redeem his terrible failure.

Not only that . . . he was *lost*.

He flew now over a land that he had never seen or heard of before. A vast country of unending grassy plains, where he saw no road or bridge or city, no camp or cookfire smoke, nor any other sign that might denote this trackless thousand-mile wilderness had ever been the habitation of men.

The directional-sphere told him he had flown into the east. This curious device, an invention of Sharajsha the Wizard, consisted of a ball of glass securely mounted to the control panel in the cabin of the floater. Within the sphere, a pendulum of metal was suspended by a thin thread. This tiny nodule of iron pointed ever to true north, by some unknown power of magic. Zandar Zan had never heard of magnetism, of course, and did not know that Sharajsha's cunning device was the world's first compass. But that was not the question.

How *far* into the east had he come?

How long had he flown, on that terrible night just past? He had entered the palace grounds at the first hour after sunfall and had seized the princess not long thereafter

. . . the collision with the Mountain of Doom had taken place just before dawn, for very shortly after boarding the second floater, Zandar Zan had seen the sun rising before him out of the unknown east. By his calculations, then, he must have piloted the floater due east for perhaps ten hours or a little less.

How fast could the airboat fly? This, of course, Zandar Zan did not know—no one knew, for no means of measuring flying speed had yet been devised. Utterly weightless because of its gravity-resisting urlium hull and fittings, the airboats of Patanga were driven by keen-bladed propellers driven by gigantic coiled springs which ran the length of the craft, from stem to stern. While it is difficult to estimate the exact power these monstrously huge springs gave, or how efficient were the rotors used in such craft, surely a weightless ship of this slim size and streamlined proportions should have been able to reach and sustain speeds of at least an hundred miles an hour. If that were true, and the craft had truly flown east for ten hours, then he had come *a thousand miles!*

His heart sank within him at the thought.

Nothing whatever was known of the lands east of the Ardath Mountains, save for vague rumor, ancient myth, and the lies of rare travelers. No maps existed of these trackless plains, and the only city of all this vast region that was inhabited by men was dreaded Zaar, the City of Black Magic. Only a fool or a madman would dream of venturing to the grim gates of that black and forbidden city of the demon-gods!

And, from all that Zandar Zan knew or had ever heard, the plains of the east were the home of the Rmoahal, those fierce fighting-men of the Nomad caravans, savage blue-skinned giants who waged endless war against each other, and whose hand was lifted in eternal enmity to all men.

Here, it was certain, Zandar Zan could find no haven. Yet—Tsargol forbidden to him—where could he go?

As he let the airboat aimlessly wander through the bright skies of noon, the Black Thief knit his brows in deep thought. Not among the barbarian Rmoahal could he find a safe haven—that was certain. Nor did he dare return to seacoast Tsargol and admit his failure. It would be like setting a death sentence on himself. Patanga, Thurdis, and Shembis were ruled by Thongor and his friends—he could not go there to find anything but a swift and bloody execution.

It was true that there were other cities in Lemuria. In his mad flight across the night sky he had passed above the city of Darundabar and perhaps over Dalakh, the easternmost city inhabited by men. In all his wanderings through the cities of the west, never once had Zandar Zan set foot in either Dalakh or Darundabar, and little or nothing did he know regarding the rulers of those cities nor the ways of life followed by their inhabitants. Perhaps he should turn the floater's needle prow west, and seek a living in one or the other of them. A thief can always make a living among men, he thought with a wry grin.

What were his alternates?

He thought. There was the city of Vozashpa, that fronted on the waves of Yashengzeb Chun the Southern Sea to the west of Dalakh . . . but no, Vozashpa was too close to Tsargol for comfort or safety. Still farther west, along the Gulf of Patanga, that mighty wedge of water that nearly split the continent of Lemuria to its heart, were the rich cities of Tarakus, where men traded in dyes and carven emeralds, and Pelorm, where men worked raw red gold and wore blue turbans for the service of the Gods, and Zangabal with its wealth of rose pearls and copper ingots, where men painted their faces green and scarlet and fought with feathered spears. But the trouble with these cities of Tarakus and Pelorm and Zangabal was that they were between Patanga the City of Fire and

Tsargol . . . too close to either one city or the other for Zandar Zan to ever sleep sound and feel secure. . . .

He must come down somewhere—and soon. He was exhausted from a night without sleep, and thirst and hunger were raging within him. But nothing did he see below on the measureless plains that tempted him to land. Indeed, everything he saw made him all the more decided on remaining aloft.

Once, in the early afternoon, he flew over a great Nomad caravan that wound across the plain like a segmented serpent of shining steel. It was a wondrous and terrible sight, the hundreds of great three-wheeled metal chariots, each as capacious as a boxcar, gorgeously ornamented with gold and flashing gems. Each of these gigantic vehicles, wherein rode the clan woman and children, was drawn by a team of three zamphs, the driver mounted on the natural horny saddle of the lead animal.

With this chain of tremendous, flat-wheeled chariots rode an escort of twenty thousand mounted warriors. The blue-skinned giants in their richly wrought and ornamented leather trappings crusted with priceless gems and rich with badges and insignia of rare metals were visions of barbaric splendor. And terrible in their savage and gorgeous might, crested with bright colored plumes, draped with fabulous cloaks of velvet and tapestried embroidery stiff with gold and silver wire, bearing their terrible war spears that measured twenty-five feet from tip to pace, they thundered by beneath his hurtling keel, mounted on long-necked swift-pacing reptiles called kroters. They boomed threats as he flew past, for they were of the fearful Zodak Horde that have no friends, and were en route to war with the lesser hordes of Shung and of Thad that roam the plains to the north. He stared with fascination at the barbaric spectacle as they passed slowly beneath him, thundering their challenge at this weird rider of the skies, shaking their enormous spears and occasionally loosing arrows at him from far below.

He flew directly over the heart of the miles-long caravan, over the gorgeous cortege of the great war chief Zarthon the Terrible himself. Zarthon rode in a stupendous chariot plated with glittering gold and his vehicle, the harness of his beasts and his own person were fantastically jeweled with a thousand flashing gems that blazed with every hue in the rainbow.

As the chariot caravan of the Zodak Horde dwindled behind, the Black Thief turned the prow of his vessel to the south. Afternoon shadows were lengthening over the plains; soon would come black night, and Zandar Zan knew he must find food and water and shelter before night fell. Already, his hunger was such that he trembled with weakness, and thirst raged within him like great fires, searing the lining of his throat and drying his mouth like old leather.

Now, although he neither knew nor cared, he flew over the broad territories claimed by the Jegga Nomads who were currently at war with their neighbors to the west, the Karzoona Clan.

Was that a city on the horizon?

His heart leaped within him, and his hands trembled on the controls. Surely it was a city! He could see the great stone roadway that led up to its gates out of the wilderness . . . then the mighty frowning walls became clear through the gathering dusk and within moments, Zandar Zan was flying above a tremendous metropolis of gray stone. Mighty buildings rolled beneath him as he slowed and hovered, circling . . . and saw that if aught still lived within the circling walls of this city, it was wild beasts and serpents. For the city lay in magnificent ruins, decayed by centuries, perhaps ages, of wind and rain. No man had dwelt within these shattered walls and roofless palaces for perhaps a thousand years. Naught ruled or roamed along these broken ways save Death, that triumphs at last over every king and over every nation ...

But—no. Men did indeed dwell here!

In the heart of the dead metropolis was that central plaza that is found in almost all of the Lemurian cities, as much common to their style of architecture as are the circling city walls themselves. And in this large square forum was gathered a mighty concourse of people around a funeral pyre—no, around two stakes that rose from heaped dry wood. It was dark now, and save for the flames of the two pyres, hard to see. Were these blue-skinned giant Rmoahal, or some lost city of man, some-how surviving in this forgotten corner of the earth a thou-sand ages past their time?

He dipped lower to investigate. ...

The shaman Tengri was furious with an icy, malignant fury that gnawed from within his heart. He had held Jomdath Jegga within his hand, and would have brought the old chief to a miserable death had not an unknown stranger erupted out of nowhere to interfere with all his well-laid plans. He nursed his crippled hand, chewing his thin lips with hatred in his heart. He had been driven from his prey by the lion, but like the jackal he bided his time and returned to the feast.

Now he rode with a dozen warriors at his back. He had made haste to return to the ruined city of Althaar where the Jegga Horde lay encamped, and there he had gathered together a band of his followers and returned swiftly to the camp of Jomdath Jegga—to find him flown, he and the mysterious warrior who had interrupted the shaman's torture of the old chief!

They had gone forth into the wilderness mounted on a great zamph. Luckily, the country to the south was barren ground and the huge three-toed footprints of the zamph could clearly be traced, even in the waning light

111

of late afternoon. Lucky, too, that Tengri and his hench-men rode swift kroters who could travel much faster than the slower and heavier zamph.

His only fear lay in the lateness of the hour. Very shortly now the great golden sun of ancient Lemuria would sink in the darkness of the west, and the footprints could no longer be followed. With impatience he urged his mount to ever greater speed. They *must* not lose the trail now. The old chief *must* not escape from his clutches a second time, for now he felt secure in his position of dominance over the Jegga clans, and knew he could safely degrade and execute the ex-chief before all the tribesmen, thus consolidating for all time his power and eliminating his old enemy and only rival claimant to the chieftainship!

Even as these thoughts were seething through his brain, one of the advance scouts shouted a warning, and he reined his beast, cantering forward to see what lay ahead.

By the dimming rays of sunset, he saw Jomdath Jegga and the unknown warrior lying trapped amidst a deadly field of gray flowers—and a dark joy flamed within his heart!

"*Hai—Jegga!*" he cried. "The Rose-of-Death has caught our quarry and holds it for us! Forward into the field, my swordsmen, and pluck our sleeping prizes from among the pretty blossoms!" He cackled with an ugly sound that was meant for laughter, but even the hardened warriors at his side, inured since the cradle to death and terror, shuddered at the dry rustle of his mirthless laughter. "Quickly, now, before the death-flowers drain them dry—and hold your breath, fools, lest you be numbed by the vapors and slumber beside them!"

Shorter than the telling was the accomplishment of the deed, and ere night fell the shaman and his warriors were on the homeward trail bearing back to the dead city of Althaar the bound and unconscious forms of Jomdath Jegga and Thongor . . . plucked from the slow death of the vampire blossoms, to be given over to a slower and more agonizing death at the fire-stakes of the Jegga Nomads in the Great Square of Althaar.

Chapter 12

THE BLACK DRAGONS—STRIKE!

The world is wide! The road is long!
On, comrades—lift our battle-song!
The day is hot! The sky is clear!
A man can die but once, I hear
   —So what's the use of fear?
   —Battle-Song of the Black Dragons

When Karm Karvus returned to Patanga from his mission to consult old Sharajsha, the wise and friendly Wizard of Lemuria, he found the city in arms and readying for war with their unknown enemy. Messengers on swift-footed kroters had borne the Red Banner to Shembis and mighty Thurdis, and the legions had gathered about the golden walls of the City of the Flame. From the cabin of his floater, as he brought it whistling low over the walls of Patanga above the heads of the great host foregathered there, Karm Karvus could make out the colors of old Barand Thon, Sark of Thurdis, and of the young Ald Turmis, Sark of Shembis. It brought joy to his heart to see so mighty a force of fighting men, sped hither to the defence of the capitol of the Sarkonate of The Three Cities!

With reckless skill, he brought the airboat down atop the roof of the palace, and raced to the Hall of Council, where he found the lords of The Three Cities awaiting his word.

The vast portals opened and he paced swiftly into the enormous hall whose marble walls were hung with gorgeous tapestries whereon were figured scenes from the hunt, from the annals of war, and the amours of the Gods.

In his silver-gilt harness, sparkling silver helmet and wide blue cloak, Karm Karvus, Daotar of the Air Guard, made a commanding and vigorous figure as he drew up at one end of the table, tore his Tsargolian rapier from its scabbard and hurled it upon the table with a thunderous crash of ringing metal. Indignation flamed in his face.

"Patangans!" he shouted. "It is mine own ancestral city of Tsargol that hath laid vile hands upon our princess! The Lord Sharajsha, who lies near death and may even at this very moment have gone to join his ancestors in the cloudy halls of Gorm the Father of Stars, hath peered into his crystal of visions and revealed that it is Tsargol makes war upon us."

There was consternation—alarm—but no sign of fear. Bluff old Mael, Lord of Tesoni, growled a rough oath, glaring and bristling with outrage. Lithe, sardonic young Prince Dru, Sumia's cousin, stroked his silken moustache with one slim finger thoughtfully—while the other hand trembled with rage, tightening on the hilt of his sword. Wise old Eodrym, Hierarch of the Temple of the Nineteen Gods, brooded grimly, his lined face weary and sad—but sternly majestic.

It was stout, red-faced old Baron Selverus who was the first to speak.

"Then it's *war*, lads—on to Tsargol! We'll teach those yellow-hearted Druids not to lay their filthy paws——!"

A tall, cloaked and helmed figure of a man of middle years turned from the window. His grizzled, close-clipped black beard was shot through with streaks of silvery gray, but otherwise the years had dealt kindly with him, for his erect figure, with its stern military bearing, was as straight and hard as a boy's. This was Zad Komis, commander of the Black Dragons, Thongor's crack regiment of seasoned warriors.

"My lords, the host of The Three Cities has been ready to march this past hour. If Tsargol is the foe, as the Daotar Karm Karvus says, then by all the Gods let us forth! Will you give the word, my Lord Mael?"

The hearty old Baron bristled with battle-lust.

"Aye, Zad Komis—let the trumpets ring loud enough to crack the sky!"

Karm Karvus' words rose above the uproar.

"My Lord Mael! Wait!"

Mael blinked. "Eh, lad? But we must be off——"

Urgency rang taut in the Air Guard's tones. "Think you, my lords, a moment more. Tsargol lies many leagues south of our city, fronting on the shores of Yashengzeb Chun the Southern Sea. It would take a day, perhaps two days, to move the host thither even if all were mounted on fast kroters. Am I not correct?"

It was Zad Komis who answered for them all.

"Aye, Daotar. But what can we do about that, except to sound the march now, and be off as swift as possible?"

Karm Karvus' reply was devastating.

"We can be at the walls of Tsargol in just hours, if we fly the entire host in airboats!"

Mael rubbed his bearded jowls, grumblingly.

"Yes, yes. . . . But—how can we lift an entire army in floaters? What about the——"

He was about to ask how the airboats could carry the might rams and siege engines, the catapults and other heavy machinery needed for war . . . and then he began dimly to perceive what Karm Karvus was talking about. So did stern Zad Komis—and his eyes flashed with excitement! Booted heels ringing on the marble pave, the tall commander of the Black Dragons strode up to the Daotar of the Air Guards and clapped him on one bare shoulder warmly.

"By all the Gods, young Karvus is *right!*" he laughed.

Old Selverus blinked in befuddlement . . . Father Eodrym seemed not to comprehend . . . even Prince Dru looked puzzled. Zad Komis grinned with a tigerish flash of bared teeth white in his brown, tanned face.

"My lords—we are still thinking in terms of war as we have known it up until now! But our Lord Thongor has changed all that, when he introduced the use of airboats at the siege of Patanga a year ago. Don't you yet realize what Karm Karvus is talking about?"

Lord Mael still looked thoughtful. The others shrugged, not yet understanding. The Lord of the Black Dragons laughed again.

"Why, look you, my lords, we have now a weapon at our command that forever renders obsolete the heavy war machines our fathers utilized. Why march men overland, even troops mounted on kroters, when the Air Guards can fly them to their destination in two or three hours! Why load slow-moving zamphs with food and supplies for a long overland march, when neither food nor supplies—nor even zamphs—are needed? Why encumber and slow down the host with all this massive paraphenalia of siege engines and battering-rams and catapults *at all?*"

Prince Dru, in his dry, mocking way, spoke up at this. "I had supposed, my lord, that such instruments were to be used in getting through the walls of an enemy city . . . am I incorrect in this assumption?"

Zad Komis laughed. "Not at all, my lord Prince—but why do we need to batter through the walls of Tsargol . . . when the Air Guards can fly over those walls?"

Then it hit them. Their eyes widened with delight, with incredulous joy.

Zad Komis turned to Karm Karvus.

"Can the Daotar of the Air Guards tell us how many warriors his fleets can transport?" he asked crisply. Karm Karvus nodded.

"We can carry, at our present strength, twenty thousand warriors and their arms," he replied.

Mael blinked shrewdly at this intelligence. "In other words," he said slowly, pondering, "the Air Guards can take on *all* of the Black Dragons, together with perhaps the company of Patangan Archers, and still have room left over for the Palace Guard and the crack troops Ald Turmis and Barand Thon brought from their cities. That still leaves behind some fifteen thousand mounted warriors. . . ."

"—Who can remain here to guard Patanga against a sneak attack!" Zad Komis summed it up.

Mael rose, wrapping a crimson cloak about his massive girth. "Then let the trumpets sound, Zad Komis, and get your Dragons aboard the floaters . . . I only hope, Karm Karvus, the power of urlium can sustain fat old Selverus and me—I'd not like to arrive at Tsargol and find the city already conquered, with no heads for my stout axe to crack!"

The trumpets rang!

No sight more majestic had the age-old walls of Patanga looked upon than the departure of the aerial army, which took place within the hour. Soaring with unearthly grandeur, a mighty fleet of airboats soared glittering in the sun, lifting over the green fields and rolling hills and arrowing through the morning air towards the seacoast city to the south.

From the cabin and prow of every craft, long banners crackled in the fresh breeze, rolling against the blue their rich heraldic fires. The plain golden field of Patanga, charged with the harsh angular Black Hawk of Valkarth was predominant, but as well the scarlet dragon on black field of great Thurdis and the green-and-silver of Shembis were to be seen.

At the controls of each craft sat one of Karm Karvus' Air Guards in silver-gilded harness and boots, sparkling helm crested with silvery wings, and the great blue sky-cloaks. But crowded to the rails, each boat bore a full complement of warriors—the Black Dragons in their jet-black trappings and black cloaks, with the terrible dragon-crested helmets; the famed Patangan Archers in cloth-of-gold, with their great war bows ready and full quivers of arrows; and troops of The Three Cities—crack regiments all!

In the vanguard of the navel fleet rode three swift ships which bore Ald Turmis of Shembis, Barand Thon of Thurdis, the Lords Selverus, Mael and Dru, as well as young Karm Karvus and his friend, Zad Komis. Beneath them sped the miles of forested Ptartha, while Karm Karvus in low tones related the full measure of what he had discovered from the great Wizard of Lemuria.

"If old Sharajsha is right—and I've never known the old magician to be wrong!—then this thief whom the black-gutted Tsargolians dispatched to carry off the lass hath failed, and neither Thongor nor Sumia are within the city, eh?" Mael rumbled questioningly.

Karm Karvus nodded. "Aye. Then there is no reason why we cannot sack Tsargol to the walls, my lord—were the Sarkaja held prisoner within, they could force us to abstain for fear of reprisals upon her person."

"I don't understand what the wizard means by saying both the Sarkon and his Princess are in the eastern lands," Mael grumbled worriedly. "I like it not—that's Rmoahal country, you know, lad, and they are dangerous folk to meddle with . . . but first things first, eh? So we level Tsargol, then worry about finding Thongor and the lass. . . ."

Like a tremendous host of silvery clouds, the aerial navy of The Three Cities flashed over the forestland and was gone to the south, where the grim walls of Tsargol rose beside the Southern Sea.

Hajash Tor had planned skillfully and well. Scouts ranging through the barren lands of Ptartha flashed word of the advancing armada by means of a cunning system of flashing mirrors, and ere the navy of Patanga had traversed half the distance to Tsargol, his army was in the field. He rode before them in a glorious gilded mail with scarlet plumes atop his gold helm, mounted on a snow-white zamph. It was his hour of triumph, and he joyed in it. Once he had been Daotarkon of Thurdis, supreme commander of the combined hosts of the Mad Sark, Phal Thurid, and of fat little Arzang Pome, Sark of Thurdis' tributary city, Shembis. He had led the mightiest host ever assembled in all the ages of ancient Lemuria to war against Patanga . . . and one single airboat had brought all his glory into the dust, and Thongor had triumphed over his army, his Sark, and over himself.

Today, he would write a glorious sequel to that dark day! Today the pride of Patanga would be vanquished into the dust, and the name of Hajash Tor would ring upon the lips of Fame. He knew it. He could almost hear it. . . .

Arzang Pome was fretful and unhappy. The squat, toad-like little man munched perfumed comfits as he rode in the gorgeous retinue of Hajash Tor; he hated activity, and loathed riding, and completely abominated warfare. Besides, he did not see why they were riding like this into the very dragon's mouth. If Thongor of Lemuria in *one* airboat had broken the host of Thurdis in a battle that had cost little Arzang Pome his throne, and almost his life, how did Hajash Tor hope to overcome a *thousand* of the damnable flying warships? Hajash Tor had not replied, when Arzang Pome fretfully put this question to him; he had merely smiled in his cold, mirthless, wolfish way, and counseled patience. . . . Arzang Pome sighed, and dug around in the box for another sweetmeat. Somehow, he just *knew* this day would end in disaster, as that other day had ended, there before the gigantic walls of Patanga.

Numadak Quelm was silent, wary, watchful. The cold fanatic eyes of the last Yellow Archdruid burned in the direction of Hajash Tor with repressed venom. Numadak Quelm had seen this Thongor bring to death his master,

Vaspas Ptol, who once had worn these robes as Hierarch of Yamath the Firegod. He had seen the mighty Valkarthan uproot the cult of Yamath, drive them forth as outlawed, homeless wanderers . . . and Numadak Quelm knew that this day would see the end of that story, this day and its outcome would decide for all time whether the cult whose last Archdruid he was would survive—or perish. And he wondered if Hajash Tor was not just an arrogant, pompous, overconfident fool . . . or if he had a secret plan with which he could truly defeat the flying ships of Patanga?

Yelim Pelorvis rode in an amber palanquin, and his thoughts were far from here. Ever since that never-forgotten day almost two years ago when Thongor of Valkarth had broken from the great arena of Tsargol, wherein he had been condemned to die, and had in his escape struck down into crimson death Drugunda Thal, last Sark of Tsargol, thus lifting Yelim Pelorvis to the heights of power over the seacoast city, he had dreamed of the Valkarthan's death. For the murder of the Sark Drugunda Thal—that was less than nothing—but Thongor had carried off the sacred Star Stone from the Tower of the Woman-Headed Serpents where it had lain enshrined for a thousand years —and for that inconceivable crime, Yelim Pelorvis had sworn the Valkarthan should die on the bloody altars of Slidith in scarlet, lingering torment as expiation for his blasphemy. But his attention drifted from the subject, as his slitted eyes became opaque . . . and as one skeletal, colorless hand dipped into a jeweled box and bore a pinch of greening powder to the priest's nostrils. The heady vaporous scent of nothlaj, the Flower-of-Dreams, rose within the veiled palanquin, and the Lord of the Red Druids felt his soul rise through scintillant realms of dream-magic borne on the odorous wings of the narcotic dust. . . .

Hajash Tor halted the host and spread the legions out in the form of a stupendous scimitar of glittering metal, curved like a crescent facing the north with the walled city of Tsargol at their backs. Within less than an hour the mighty fleet of a thousand airboats would come soaring and flashing into view . . . and then he would strike!

He cast a glance behind him at the great zamph-teams, yoked to massive wooden wains. Scurrying druids were unpacking from these wooden carts mysterious globes of fragile black glass. From the baggage trains, a row of huge catapults were moving up according to Hajash Tor's carefully preconceived plans. Even as he watched with gloating eyes, the spheres of glass were gently, carefully loaded into the cupped hands of the giant catapults. And Hajash Tor laughed silently to himself, remembering.

Two years ago in Thurdis, he had watched as wise old Oolim Phon tested his new invention, the airboat, and had listened as the canny old alchemist explained how the magic powers of urlium, the synthetic gravity-resisting metal he had isolated and perfected, could be nullified.

"There is one substance known that can destroy the power of urlium," the old alchemist had explained in his quavering voice. "All the lifting power of the airboat's hull is negated at the touch of this substance, and for *ten hours* the craft cannot lift, but lies mired with heavy weight upon the bosom of the earth. . . ."

Hajash Tor grinned wolfishly. This useful item of information he had tucked away, against some future day when it might come into value. And now that day had dawned! The rare mineral that old Oolim Phon had named to him now lay in powdered form within those globes of delicate glass. And when the aerial armada of Patanga came soaring over their heads, and he gave the signal that would send those glass bombs hurtling into the sky, to smash into atoms against the urlium hulls. . . .

He grinned again.

He could hardly wait to see it.

Chapter 13

FORTRESS OF WIZARDRY

"... and far to the east, the black walls of Zaar the City of Magicians yet rose inviolate, wherein ruled the black wizards who worshipped with terrible rites the Third Lord of Chaos, Thamungazoth, the Lord of Magic. Here, through the long ages since the fall of Nemedis and the first kingdoms of Man, the Black Magicians had brooded over their dark lore, biding their time to strike. . . ."

—The Lemurian Chronicles

Princess Sumia came to full awareness slowly, as one who awakens from the drugged trance of some magic vapor. At first she could not think where she was, nor how she had come into this strange place. Indeed, her mind was as blank as a parchment scroll wherein naught has yet been enscribed, or whereon that which was written has been erased. She had been with Shangoth the Nomad . . . they were returning to the camp of Jomdath Jegga, his father . . . when. . . .

But, no, she could not recall. They had walked astray from the path, had they not? Dimly . . . dimly, she remembered a weird tower of black glass rising like an arm of ebony, holding in its black claws a great crystal that flashed and glittered and beckoned. . . .

She remembered all—and looked around her desperately!

She stood in a dark chamber, high-vaulted and almost devoid of illumination. She was bound to a column of black glass that seemed to grow up out of the vitreous floor like a stalagmite of dark obsidian. Or—no, she was not exactly bound, for her hands were free and unfettered: it was just that she could not remove them from the column. They were pressed, palms down, flat against the rough cold glass, and strive as she might, she could not lift them from the grip of whatever magical force held her imprisoned . . . no more than can an iron filing pull itself free of the power of a magnet. Only her hands were affected, oddly enough, the rest of her slim body did not adhere to the glass pillar.

The remainder of the room conformed to the same eerie illusion of having *grown* to its form in some weird organic way, rather than having been raised by manlabor. The floor was uneven, rising into the walls at the edges of the room; the walls themselves slanted and curved like the cells of a honeycomb, rather than flat planes. As for the arched ceiling, she could see little detail above, for the groined roof was lost in thick shadow.

In the center of the room a glowing circle was traced against the black, glassy floor. It glowed with cold green fires like the phosphorescent eyes of great cats, burning against the blackness. Within the circle stood a great throne chair of ancient wood, thick-carven with uncouth hieroglyphics of some unknown, antique tongue. Beside this chair was a pedestal or reading stand of the same age-darkened wood, supporting a massive book which lay open as if ready for some rite or service. The leaves of this book were not of paper, not even of parchment, but of *metal* . . . a thin sheeted metal of some greenish silver alloy such as Sumia had never seen or heard of, flexible as paper, yet enduring the ages. Upon the metal leaves, great complex symbols were embossed with metallic, glowing inks . . . weird designs traced in scarlet, ebon black, sulphur yellow and indigo. The colored designs shimmered, casting a flickering spectrum of light about the great book, and the very air about it throbbed to the vibration of some unknown force locked within those cryptic symbols. Although Sumia did not know it, this was *Sardathmazar*, the Book of Power.

The light from the phosphorescent circle was brightening. By its eerie illumination, she suddenly saw Shangoth. The blue-skinned giant was bound with the invisible force that imprisoned her, it seemed, although his station was across the room. His head was sunken upon his mighty chest, but he was not unconscious as was her first thought, for almost as soon as she saw him, the Nomad lifted his head and spoke to her from the length of the dark chamber.

"Courage!" he said calmly.

Sumia nodded and tried to smile, although her heart was heavy. She tried to think how Thongor would behave under grim circumstances such as these. She knew he would say: I still live, and while I live, I hope.

Suddenly a man stood within the circle of green radiance.

He had not been there a moment before, nor had Sumia seen him enter the room. Her blood chilled at the uncanny manner in which he had melted out of thin air. It was as if the darkness had congealed, thickening into a dense cloud, forming into the likeness of a very tall man in a complicated garment of many-folded cloth. He stood looking at her with mocking, sardonic eyes that glittered from a pale, strong face like fragments of burning ice. Then he seated himself in the throne-chair and spoke in a harsh, low voice, filled with echoes of irony and cold laughter: a voice that grated upon her nerves, and tore at the fabric of her composure.

"I greet the Princess Sumia, daughter of the House of Chond and Sarkaja of Patanga and The Three Cities! And the Prince Shangoth, son of Jomdath, chieftain of the Jegga Nomads. Long has it been since my bastion welcomed within its gates guests of such lineage and nobility!"

Shangoth replied for the two of them.

"Seldom are guests bound by their host like chained animals," he said with simple dignity. The tall man laughed mockingly.

"Bound, you say? I see no shackles! You may move if you like, Nomad—what, you prefer not to move, eh? Then do not complain of my hospitality."

Sumia lifted her small head proudly and looked him in the eye unflinchingly.

"You know that we are chained with magic; must you mock us as well? In my country, prisoners are treated better than you treat guests!"

He smiled calmly, settling back in his chair. Light grew brighter, pulsing from the open grimoire on the reading-stand. It painted his cold features with satanic colored fires.

"Ah! Your country. Yes . . . we have become very interested in your country of the west, of late. We must speak of it—but come, this is no way for a gracious host to act. I have not introduced myself!"

"Pray do so," Sumia said coolly. "I would know to whose 'courtesy' I owe the discomfort of these magic bonds."

He bowed slightly, ironically, remaining seated.

"My name is Adamancus, a magus of the city of Zaar and a lord of its councils. I am the Guardian of the Northern Marches, and from this bastion, like an outpost, I keep watch on the lands where roam the troublesome hordes of the Rmoahal . . . and occasional chance visitors, such as yourself, lovely lady."

"Thank you. I shall remember your name," Sumia replied. He lifted his eyebrows with mock surprise.

"Indeed? Well, more of that later, my lady. We were speaking of your kingdom of Patanga . . . ah, yes, that name has come up often before the Council of the Nine Archimages in recent times. We are becoming increasingly—ah, *concerned* with what is happening in your western land. We are, in fact, not pleased with the recent turn of events. I refer to this upstart adventurer, Thongor of Valkarth—whose bride and queen I perceive you to be, my lady."

She started, just a trifle. "Thongor? What have you to do with him?"

He shrugged. "Little or nothing—as yet. But the time is coming, when we shall have to, ah, meddle just a bit with his growing little empire, before it becomes more of an inconvenience to us. Already, in fact, certain plans of ours concerning you of the west have gone awry because of this adventurer and his little empire. Ah, yes. . . . Something shall have to be done. . . ." He fell silent, brooding thoughtfully, his pointed chin resting on one balled fist whereon talismanic gems and ensorcelled rings flashed and glittered.

Puzzled, Sumia ventured a question as to what plans of Zaar Thongor had bent awry. He mused grimly, lips tightening.

"This oafish barbarian came first to our notice no more than eighteen months ago. Our mighty Lords and tutors in the Black Sciences, the dread *Narghasarkaya* whom you of the west call the 'Dragon Kings' and who ruled all of this Earth for millions of years before the creation of Phondath the Firstborn and the coming of Men, were foiled by this upstart Northlander in their stupendous plot to open a Portal to Beyond through which the Chaos Lords we both worship and serve might manifest Themselves here on the Plane of Material Creation. By his interference, the work of a thousand ages was undone and the thaumaturgic power of the Dragon Kings ruined for all the ages of time to come . . ."

Sumia's mind reeled at the terrific import of this discovery! The Dragon Kings, a long-lived race of serpent beings who had dominated the planet during the Age of Reptiles, had at last broken before the might of the First Kingdoms of Man. Their strength sapped during The Thousand Year War, they were slaughtered. Only a few of the malignant

Dragon Lords managed to elude the triumphant First Men. They fled to the Inner Sea of Neol-Shendis, hidden away in the mountainous heart of the continent, and there for centuries they rested, letting their power grow, while their cold reptilian brains conceived of an ultimate evil: the summoning into the universe of the terrible Black Gods of Chaos whom the Nineteen Gods had cast into eternal exile beyond the stars in the supernal moment of Creation. The final, ultimate and cataclysmic Rite of Conjuration Thongor had interrupted, for the mightiest magician of the age, Sharajsha, had enlisted his aid to destroy the scheme of the Dragon Kings. But now, two years after this event, to learn that the Dragon Kings had nurtured and infected *men* with their blasphemous worship of ultracosmic Evil was a fantastic revelation! But before her mind could do aught but explore the first implications of this intelligence, Adamancus was speaking again.

"And then, ere we who are the children and students of the Dragon Kings had more than begun to absorb the impact of this devastating failure, and lay our own plans for the restoration of the Dark Gods—this same barbarian struck another mighty blow against our cause. 'Twas in the west, a portion of the world in which we had little interest, thinking it secure enough under the domination of our brothers of the black cults of the Firegod and the Lord of Blood. One of the mightiest of our order, a magus of that same Council of the Nine whereto I as well am member, had been given the mastery of the west . . ."

"What . . . man . . . was he?" Sumia faltered.

"In the west he was named Thalaba the Destroyer; here, we knew him by another name, but that is of no matter."

Again, Sumia was shaken—Thalaba the Destroyer!

Well did she remember that hideous, ghoul-like and loathsome being whose dark arts had enslaved the brain of Phal Thurid, driving him to madness with whispered temptations, setting a fire within his heart until he burned with lust for power, with the insane ambition to conquer and overwhelm all of the cities of the west, welding them into one warlike empire, with himself as Lord of the West.

Sumia's blood ran cold at the very memory of that black-cloaked thing whose name spelt dread and terror to the warriors of Thurdis. It had been Thalaba who had goaded the drug-maddened Sark to set siege to Patanga—and now she began to perceive why this had been done, since Patanga had come under the power of the Yellow Druids who had seized the kingdom for themselves, forcing her into exile. At first thought, this might seem odd—the Yellow Druids were allied to the Black City of Zaar, and Thalaba, now revealed as a Lord of Zaar, set Phal Thurid, his pawn, in war *against* the Druids. But now it came to her that the Druids had overreached their place in Zaar's plan for the west, had sought to replace even the primacy of Zaar itself!

So it was, she mused, with those whose minds are perverted to the worship of evil, that they are corrupted in every way, even in their loyalties to their brothers in the same Dark Cause. . . .

But Thalaba's attempt to whelm and grind down Patanga had failed—disastrously, as it happened, in that Thurdis itself was whelmed and broken when Thongor struck, and thus at one blow both the Druids and Thalaba of Zaar were undone! No wonder the Black Magicians of the east entertained desires to wreck a grim vengeance against her beloved mate!

But this was astounding news . . . so Thalaba the Destroyer had been more than he seemed—had been, in fact, a secret emissary of Zaar the Black City of Magicians half a world away! This was amazing news . . . but the Mage Adamancus was speaking again, musing half-aloud, as if he had forgotten they were present.

"And so your Thongor came meddling in, and all our plans were disturbed—seriously disturbed. And the lord Thalaba was slain during this Thongor's disruption of the siege of Patanga, and the Council of Nine became the

Council of Eight, and one pole of our power was irretrievably gone, and all our strength was lessened. . . ."

He lifted his burning eyes again and fixed them on the bound and helpless girl who stood before him, her slim white limbs gleaming through the tatters of her robe, pallid against the rough black glass of the pillar to which she was held by bands of enchantment.

"Ah—but that was not all. No, this Thongor has since been busily at work throughout the west, uprooting the cult of the Lord of Flame from Patanga and driving forth into outlawry our brothers in the service of Chaos. And now, I fear me our brothers of the cult of the Lord of Blood have touched off war between Tsargol and Patanga by their ill-planned abduction of your royal self, my lady . . . and that will bring the warlike Valkarthan barbarian down upon them with sword and torch, to set all their kingdom afire unless they are far more clever than I give them credit for being . . . they were fools, fools not to consult us, their elder brothers and superiors in the service of Chaos! And I fear they shall pay most richly for that grievous error!"

Sumia caught her breath, and went pale. "War?" she echoed faintly. "War between Patanga and Tsargol?"

"Aye," he nodded, his voice somber. "Even at this moment, I believe your very interesting flying fleets are hurtling against Hajash Tor's secret weapon . . . but let us see for ourselves, shall we, my lady?"

He stood, tall and dark, and drew from a desk of black metal that stood behind his chair a curious instrument. It was all sparkling crystal spheres and spirals of silvery wire, clustered at one end of a long staff of copper bound with rings of some unknown black substance Sumia could not at a glance identify. Adamancus did something to the handle of this piece of magical apparatus, and searing electric-blue fire blazed up within the hollow spheres, where weirdly-twisted wire filaments were intricately set between electrodes.

Adamancus pointed this metal staff towards the far side of the room and spoke a thunderous phrase in some harsh, terrific language that Sumia had never heard. It was not a tongue such as the mouths of men are shaped to speak, and it rang like a roll of metallic thunder through the vaulted room, and the glinting obsidian floor shook to the seismic rhythm of its awful syllables.

The further wall of the room melted into gray light!

A fantastic blur of rushing, wheeling shapes burst into Sumia's astonished gaze. Her lips parted in a gasp of incredulous amazement. An oath was wrung from Shangoth's lips, and the mighty blue-skinned warrior called on his Gods in an anguished voice, shaken before the marvel of this spectacular act of magic. The cold, mocking voice of Adamancus lifted above their cries, ringing with mirthful laughter.

"Fear not, my guests, fear not! It is an illusion only—a simple trick of captured light, which collapses distance, bringing the likeness of far things near—to the sight alone, of course. But watch—*see*——"

Now the whirling shadow-shapes drew into sharper focus, although still there were no colors. All was depicted in tones of black and white and gray, which lent a strange unreality to this mirror of far-off things. Sound, too, was missing—and so strange was the moving picture of light and shade that at first Sumia's eye could not sort out the images and match them with the remembered realities they stood for.

But soon she saw clearly. It was as if the entire wall had evaporated, and they looked forth, from some towering and incredible height, upon the curved face of the great Earth itself. There was Patanga at the head of the Gulf, that tiny cluster of miniscule structures ringed in with a thick wall . . . then her eyes followed the long curve of meadow and hill and forest down to Tsargol on the seacoast. It was astounding, this magic vision that probed through space! Their point of vantage must have been a thousand miles above the earth, for so great a section of the continent to be encompassed in so small a space. Yet the vision was clearer and sharper than the reality would have been, had they in truth been raised a thousand miles aloft.

And there, midway between the two cities, majestically soaring over the great forests of Ptartha, came drifting on a stupendous fleet of flying craft, rank after gleaming rank of them, fluttering with banners and bristling with warriors, floating across the face of the world with incredible velocity, and moving in utter silence, like a flying army of shadowy ghosts. It was true—Patanga and Tsargol at war!

"This—this vision—shows truly what is happening at this very moment in time, half-way across the continent of Lemuria?" Sumia asked, faintly. The black magician nodded, then flicked some control set in the end of his metallic staff. The electric fires died within the crystal spheres that crested the strange instrument—and the magical vision winked out of existence upon the instant. Sumia felt her pulses thunder with tension and excitement. *War!* And she was here, far from her homeland. And Thongor— where was he in this hour? And against what "secret weapon" were the aerial legions of The Three Cities hurling themselves?

As suddenly as it had sprung into being, the vision died —faded in a ghost of gray light and was gone, plunging the room into blackness again. Adamancus switched off the blazing power within his magic instrument, blue flames dying, and replaced the weird object in the metal desk behind his chair.

"We shall not wait to see the gorgeous spectacle, when the invincible fleets of the City of the Flame come up against the magnificent weapon Hajash Tor has ready for them," said Adamancus in his mocking, laughter-filled way, "for, as your host, I dare not violate the sacred laws of hospitality by subjecting my guests to so terrible an experience. No . . . you and I, my lady, have more important business together."

Shangoth growled deep in his throat, and mighty thews swelled and writhed along his massive shoulders as he fought against the invisible magic bonds. But Sumia did not shrink nor falter before the half-veiled menace in Adamancus' tones. She drew herself up proudly, like the queen she was, and looked at him with a cold, contemptuous glance.

"We have *no* business, wizard, and I command you to set us free and let go go upon our way."

He smiled, but his mocking gaze grew thoughtful.

"It occurs to me," he mused, appraising her with a measuring eye, "that I could gain a superb revenge against this Thongor. . . ."

Shangoth roared, "If you lay one hand on the princess, you filth-hearted sorcerer, you had best slay me. For I swear by the eternal Gods of Sky that I will tear that hand off and crush your heart with it——"

Adamancus did not even seem to hear the Nomad's wrathful threat. He was thinking. . . .

"If I were to steal your soul and mind from your body, and set therein in place of those an Elemental conjured from the nighted deep and sworn to my service . . . then permit you to leave, to rejoin your barbarian lover . . . what an amusing game it would be!"

Despair thrust a needle of ice through her heart . . . and Sumia realized the magician did not jest.

CHAPTER 14

THE SIGN OF THE GODS

Upas wood and Mandrake weed,
  Juice of hemlock, lotus seed,
Living heart of Unicorn
  Slaughtered in the mists of morn,
Mix to the chanting of a rune
  Mix in the fullness of the Moon . . .
  —*Shaman's Song*

The great golden moon of lost Lemuria glared down on a primitive spectacle of barbaric savagery.

Its golden rays lit with an eerie radiance the awesome ruins of the aeons-old city of Althaar. Where once a mighty people of Earth's remotest dawn had risen and reigned, now the stately palaces and hoary temples were given over to grim savages devoid of culture, a people without a past, a rude nation dominated by cruelty.

In the half-wrecked square of the ancient city, the Jegga Nomads prepared to burn alive Thongor and their deposed and exiled chief, Jomdath Jegga. The stakes were set up, blackened poles of tough arld wood whose charred appearance gave mute testimony to the many times they had been put to the same grim use ere now. Great mounds of dry brush were heaped about these stakes, and Nomad warriors were even now chaining to these poles their exiled chief and the strange outlander the shaman had taken with him. Thongor saw that these chains were of iron, and his heart sank within him, although he allowed no flicker of emotion to alter by a hair's breadth the impassive set of his features. If die he must, he could at least show these warriors how a North-lander could die without a sound.

Perhaps it would have been a kinder death to have fallen before the vampiric thirst of those gray hell-flowers, he thought grimly. In the embrace of their narcotic perfume, he and the heroic old chief would have sunk ever deeper into a drugged slumber from which there would have been no awakening, but also no pain. But what use to dwell on those things that cannot be helped? The vengeful shaman had pursued closely on their tracks, rescuing them from the death-dealing blossoms only to give them over to another death, bound to the fire-stakes before howling savages. He resolved to die without affording the Nomads the amusement of watching a strong man break before the lash of terror.

He watched the throng, as he had done ever since recovering consciousness slowly from the spell of the dream-inducing flowers. He had watched while the shaman haranged them, cowed them with his sorcerous powers, and convinced them that it was the will of the Sky-Gods they sacrifice the exiled, outlawed ex-chief together with the outlander of strange race and unknown origins who had sought to carry him off. Neither Jomdath nor Thongor, of course, had been permitted to argue their defense. And at length the cunning shaman had so whipped the Nomads' spirits by playing upon their superstitious fears, that he had persuaded them against their own reluctance to break Clan-law and bring to death their chief whose life at their hands should have been sacred. Tengri's performance was a masterpiece of devilish eloquence. He had triumphed at last.

Within moments now, the leaping Rmoahal savages would apply their burning torches to the brush-heaps, and the ordeal would begin. But Thongor half-sensed that the shaman was not as secure in his place of power as he may have believed, for traces of the old loyalty seemed to lurk within many hearts. Thongor glimpsed some whose expressions were tinged with shame, with half-hearted reluctance, with even a faint glow of admiration for the faultless courage and nobility that Jomdath Jegga had shown this hour. For, during the long speech the shaman had made, not once did the exiled chief flinch or tremble. He stood straight and tall, his face stamped with cold contempt, iron pride, unwavering and undaunted even in the very jaws of death. Thongor felt that more than a few present would have rejoiced in setting Jomdath free, and chaining the hate-maddened shaman Tengri in his fiery place.

And in the meanwhile, the Valkarthan nurtured within him a spark of hope. For one slim chance at escape had occurred to him, and behind the stolid mask of his grim-set features, his mind was racing, tumbling with agile plans. These shackles had been wrought to fit the wrists of a Rmoahal giant . . . and the Rmoahal towered over Thongor, and their arms were of greater girth than his own, in correspondence to their greater size!

Was there just the faintest wisp of a chance, that by a supreme exertion he could tear his wrists free?

Not while the gloating eyes of a thousand armed warriors were fixed on his every move, hoping to see him squirm with terror at the first, and then with intolerable agony. . . .

But if their attention could be diverted?

Perhaps. If not, well . . . then Father Gorm would welcome the spirit of another Valkarthan warrior to his mighty hearth, when the winged War Maids bore across the skies to the Hall of Heroes the soul of Thongor.

Now the time was short. The shaman Tengri had made his foul invocation to the death-spirits, and advanced towards the two fire-blackened stakes whereon Jomdath and the Northlander were chained, bearing aloft in his dagger-crippled hand a flaming torch. The expression of gloating lust cut deep on the shaman's fleshless features roused Thongor's disgust. If a man must be slain, give him

135

a clean swift death with cold steel, but this lingering death, roasting in chains like a trapped animal was degrading to the Barbarian's simple humanity . . .

Gathering all eyes, the shaman lifted the burning torch —flourished it to the Eleven Directions and the Seven Winds—and lowered it to the waiting brush, in an aching silence.

—That broke in an astounded chorus of shouts!

"A sign! A sign! The Sky-Gods bring doom upon us for daring to lift our hands against the sacred chief!"

Even Thongor's grim features lost their rigidity, as he lifted his eyes to see the astonishing thing in the skies— and he voiced a grunt of surprise at the omen from Heaven!

It would seem that Father Gorm was not yet ready to play host to his spirit in the Hall of Heroes. He smiled in savage joy, and now that not a single eye in all that crowded square was upon him or any other thing save for the stupendous miracle in the heavens, he gave a mighty effort, and tore his hands free of the over-large shackles. They came free with some difficulty, and Thongor left a few square inches of skin behind. It was, he thought, a small price to pay for the freedom of his hands. Again, he lifted his head to stare at the vision that had descended upon the city from the night-dark skies.

The silvery gleaming hull of the floater had drifted down over the square, circling slowly while Zandar Zan peered from the cabin, scrutinizing the scene below. What curious and fortuitous mischance had caused Thongor's deadly enemy to arrive at this crucial moment was beyond reckoning, but the ironic tricks of Fate had made Thongor's foe his miraculous rescuer.

His unexpected appearance over the great square drove the Rmoahal throng into panic. Instantly, they interpreted the aerial apparition as a sign from the Gods that Jomdath Jegga was to be spared, and a score of the brawny Nomad warriors plunged into the flames to free the old chief.

Tengri screamed above the crowd, seeking to overawe them, but his spell was broken, and he was brushed aside without ceremony. His henchmen sprang to his side, steel flashed in the firelight, and the throng erupted in battle. Thongor was not needed here, so he struck like lightning.

From the afterdeck rail still dangled the grapnel-hook that was the airboat's anchor, hanging from a length of stout cordage. Thongor recalled how he had moored the craft by securing the grapnel to the cliff. When the Black Thief had leaped aboard the empty airboat, he had tugged the line loose, never bothering to draw it aboard again. Now as the airboat circled low, Thongor crouched and sprang into the air, his mighty muscles hurling him skywards in a lithe bound. Every ounce of strength went into that mighty leap, for the Valkarthan knew he would have but this one chance—already the airboat was lifting out of the square. The steely muscles of his long lithe legs drove against the earth like coiled springs, thrusting him into the air with terrific force.

One outstretched hand brushed the grapnel-hook—slipped—and clung with an unbreakable grip like iron.

The airboat's sharp prow knifed the cold air, lifting sharply on a steep incline. It soared up out of the square and vanished into the night, with the Valkarthan warrior dangling from the end of the line.

In the square below, the henchmen of the shaman were overwhelmed by sheer weight of numbers, disarmed and bound. Jomdath, now free, was the center of a vast crowd of shouting warriors who hailed him as chief and lord of the Jegga Horde, knelt before him, offering their swords. It was a scene of barbaric grandeur, the proud old chief standing in his glittering trappings, surrounded by chanting, kneeling warriors with nodding plumes and gem-encrusted harness, their lifted swords flashing in the orange light of the burning pyres that cast a wild and wavering illumination on the crumbling marble façades of the age-old palaces that lined the wreckage-littered square. He accepted their homage proudly, and when they demanded of him to what end the captive shaman should be sent, a grim smile touched the noble grandeur of his impassive features. He smiled at Tengri, who, held by a dozen warriors, fought madly like some ferocious beast brought at last to bay, his gaunt skull-face contorted with inhuman rage, foam dripping from his snarling jaws, his eyes glaring from side to side, catching the fire-light like the burning orbs of some great jungle cat.

"Were I as cruel as he, I should give the devil-worshipping wizard over to the flames, to be bound to yonder stake in my place and to suffer the fiery torments that he decreed for me. But this penalty I reserve, should ever he seek to come amongst the Horde again. Nay . . . I shall deliver him unto the first doom to which he sent my son and me!" And calling a young warrior who had been in the retinue of Shangoth and still was loyal to the prince, the old chief commanded: "Jugrim! Take a score of warriors and escort the shaman and those who follow him to the edge of the city, and set them afoot into the wilderness, to wander where they will and live amidst the waste however they may, not to return amongst us upon pain of death at the fire-stakes. Begone!"

And as the old chief received the plaudits of his people, it was done. In a single hour, the shaman Tengri had fallen from the utmost heights of triumph and power, to be thrust forth into the nighted plain to suffer there a lonely and miserable fate, the same to which he had sent Jomdath of the Jegga Nomads.

Thongor swung at the end of the rope like a pendulum, the winds howling about him like banshees in the cold darkness of night. The golden moon had hidden its bright face behind a veil of tattered cloud and the night was plunged into a darkness as black as pitch.

They were flashing through the night at furious speed.

The ruins of Althaar were lost behind in darkness, and now the steeply-climbing airboat was soaring aloft some thousand feet or more above the level tundra. It was heading south, although Thongor could not tell, for Zandar Zan had decided he could find no rest nor supplies nor safe haven in the dead city wherein howling savages fought and slew one another, and was seeking elsewhere.

Cold wind whipped Thongor's bare body as he swung helplessly through space. His unshorn mane streamed out behind him on the shrieking blast like some tattered war-banner. The huge crimson cloak swelled from his broad shoulders like the wings of some gigantic bat. He began slowly to climb up the rope hand over hand. His sword had been taken from him when the shaman Tengri had captured him amid the field of death-flowers, and he was unarmed. But with bare hands alone he resolved to break the Black Thief and hurl him to the earth far below . . .

The floater swung a little as Thongor stole silently over the rail and gained the afterdeck, but Zandar Zan did not notice. He sat in the pilot's chair, hunched over the controls, staring out into the night. He did not know that he had involuntarily taken aboard a passenger, until he heard a low laugh behind him. He spun—to see the terrific apparition of Thongor standing in the cabin's low door. The great bronzed body of the warrior, clad in black leather harness, crouched as if to spring at his throat, and in a flashing instant of terror, the Tsargolian knew that this was none other than Thongor himself.

Thongor laughed again, harshly, low in his throat. His strange golden eyes burned in his scarred, tanned face, like the eyes of some beast of the night. He stepped within the cabin.

But Zandar Zan moved as swiftly as a striking snake. One black-gloved hand flashed within his cloak and emerged, holding a long slim dagger poised for throwing. It was an assassin's weapon, and one with which Zandar Zan had long since become adept. Thongor halted as the slim needle of steel flashed into view, and now it was the Thief's turn to laugh. For Thongor was bare-handed and without a weapon.

Or was he?

As his great hands grasped futilely against the empty leather of his scabbards, his fingers brushed against a bulky object stuffed within his pouch. A memory shot into his mind—the strange magical gem with which the shaman Tengri had threatened him many hours ago, back in the camp of Jomdath.

His hands were a blur, so swiftly did Thongor strike. Zandar Zan had the speed and agility of an assassin, but Thongor's were the hair-trigger nerves of a fighting warrior—the weird gem sparkled as it hurled across the swaying cabin. It struck the thief's shoulder ere even he could hurl the knife. And, as it touched his body, terrific sparks of green-gold electric fire sparkled from it!

Steel rang on steel, as the dagger dropped from Zandar Zan's lifeless hands. The touch of the green crystal had numbed him from fingertip to shoulder with a lightning-flash of tingling force. And Thongor sprang.

But at that moment, a gust of wind caught the unpiloted airboat. Before the buffeting gale, the needle-prow swerved, hurling Thongor against the wall. And Zandar Zan, clutching his strengthless arm that still tingled numbly from the paralyzing touch of the magic electric crystal, darted past Thongor to the deck beyond.

His self-control had snapped at last. Panic had seized him, and the foolish move to the swaying, open deck was his undoing. For again the wind seized the hurtling floater —the deck swayed sickeningly—Zandar Zan staggered backward, his knees striking the low rail—and with a terrible cry he pitched over into the black night and was gone, falling like a stone to a swift, merciful death far below.

Thus perished the Thief of Tsargol.

Thongor wasted little time in gaining control of the airboat, lifting her above the level of the storm. Nor did he waste thought on the dead thief, for, warrior that he was, sudden death was an old companion of the Valkarthan, and a simple shrug was all the eulogy he spent on Zandar Zan.

And then terror struck!

What was that coil of glowing vapor that swirled within the little cabin? The hair on Thongor's nape prickled as he watched something melt out of emptiness behind his chair . . . a glowing phantom formed into the shadowy likeness of a tall, majestic old man leaning on a staff, his bearded visage oddly familiar. A sudden oath was wrung from Thongor in utter astonishment.

"*Sharajsha!* Old friend—is it you?" he growled.

The ghostly figure nodded.

"Do you live—or are you a phantom come from the cold halls of the restless dead?"

Although the phantom's lips did not move, a thin echoing voice filled the cabin with its eerie whisper.

"Death claims me even now, O Thongor! Yet, whilst I yet linger a time upon the earth plane, I have detached my Body-of-Light to seek you out in your far place. Fly swift, my warrior friend, in the direction that even now you take, for your princess lies in deadly danger . . . aye, in a danger more terrible than mere death! For a Black Magician of Zaar hath her enchained within the uppermost chamber of his ebon tower and seeks, even now, to summon an Elemental Demon to inhabit her body. . . . Swift, my friend, to her rescue, and may the eternal blessing of the everlasting Gods be with you in this hour, and all the hours of your life!"

The bodiless whispering voice died and the shadowy figure of the old enchanter lifted his staff in a salute of farewell . . . then melted into formless, swirling vapor again. Thongor blinked, and behold! the apparation was gone as utterly as if it had never been.

So death had come at last for his ancient friend! Once

he had saved Thongor from death at the fangs of a jungle dragon. Once they had fought together side by side in a mighty struggle to defeat the last, lingering remnants of the Dragon Kings . . . and long had the great Wizard of Lemuria with his ageless wisdom and magical lore held back the remorseless destiny that all men face. But now, even his tremendous science could no longer shield him from the shadows, and death had come to the great Sharaj-sha as it comes to all men at last.

But Thongor had no time now to mourn the passing of his old friend. Sumia was in danger and Thongor bent swiftly to the controls, urging the last atom of speed from the airboat that clove the rain-swept skies as swiftly as a steel arrow. His grim gaze was bent ahead, searching the dark earth for a sign of that black tower wherein his princess lay helpless before a menace that sought to steal forth her very soul and give her young body over to the domination of a terrible demon summoned from the light-less pits of the utmost hell.

The glittering airboat cleft the stormy skies of ancient Lemuria, tracing a gleaming path down the night like a shooting star, as Thongor raced against time to his goal.

Would he arrive in time?

Could he?

Chapter 15

THE LAST INCANTATION

Seek not, O Mage, to raise the Demons of
the Pit . . . for they will turn and rend thee.
　　　　　　　　　—The Scarlet Edda

Adamancus of Zaar set about the dark ritual without delay. First, with a pointed Rod of Power, he traced a lumi-
nous circle about the column whereto Sumia was held
helpless in the invisible bonds. Another such circle he set
about Shangoth. These protective circles of phosphorescent flame would shield his two prisoners from harm at
the claws of the Elemental, for once he had conjured up
the being, only the protective circles could shield any living thing from the fiend's rage. Such a circle, of course,
encompassed his own throne chair and reading-stand:
were even he to venture beyond the shielding circle, no
power on earth could arm him against the Elemental's
wrath.

And once the demon was sworn to him and had yielded
to his mastery, he would break the circle that protected
Sumia, and the Elemental could enter, to seize her body
and devour her soul. The devil-possessed princess Adamancus would then release, so that she might return to
Thongor. The meddling barbarian, of course, would never
suspect that the lovely body of his mate no longer housed
her pure young soul, but was now inhabited by a black
thing drawn up from the nethermost Abyss. With the de-
mon-possessed princess a puppet to his will, the Black
Magician could then use her as a tool wherewith to wreak
a terrible doom upon Thongor, his growing young empire,

and all of the helpless peoples of the west. Adamancus smiled at the thought, and began his grisly preparations. . . .

Having set in place the circles of protection, he next kindled a Hell Flame on a low altar of black emerald. The weird crimson flame smoldered a few inches above the upper surface of the gemlike substance, feeding upon no fuel that mortal eyes could ascertain. Its scimitar-like flames of molten scarlet writhed and danced with a hypnotic and ophidian grace, luring the gaze of Shangoth and of Sumia. Here was danger, so Adamancus used great care: unless held under conscious control of his pentacles of Power, the all-devouring Flame could burst with ease its limits, and would consume every atom of his enchanted bastion before returning to its ultra-telluric abode.

Now was he ready to begin the last ritual. Arming himself with potent talismans whereon terrific runes of Elder Lore were graven deep on pendent disks of rarest orichalc and precious jazite, the magic metal of Lemuria, he began the great conjuration. Spread open before him on its mighty stand, the imperishable metallic leaves of *Sardathmazar*, the Book of Power, throbbed with vibrant energies, and the complex multi-figured symbols traced thereon in glowing inks cast an opal glow, lighting his pale strong features as he bent above the mighty book.

He chanted a series of names in that uncouth language of the magi for which the lips of men were never shapen to speak. The earth-shaking force of those names rung through the vaulted black chamber and shook the very tower to its massy base.

Then he began chanting in the common tongue which both Shangoth the Nomad and Sumia of Patanga knew: the one language universal to all men of this remote age. The dread Powers he invoked made the smoky, flame-lit air of the chamber seethe with currents of force.

"By the River of Fire and the River of Blood! It is the Hour of Sassur, the Ninth Hour of the Night, and the

Moon stands in her Twelfth Mansion, the Mansion of Al-zarpha, whereover ruleth the Intelligence Abdizuel! And the Moon sits in the Zodiacal House of the Lion, where-over ruleth the Intelligence Verchiel! Now by the Great Name Shamain the Heaven of the Moon, and by the Name of Arcan the Intelligence who ruleth over the Spirits of the Air upon this day, do I summon thee! Come, by the Supernal Powers of Abdizuel, Verchiel, Shamain, Arcan..."

The thunderous invocation rose, shaking the room with the seismic impact of these terrific Names of Power . . . and there before the very eyes of Shangoth and the Princess, a smoky wraith began to form out of empty air!

Like spirals and whorls of green vapor it coiled glow-ingly against the darkness. Tentacles of emerald mist swam through the dim air, serpentine writhing limbs that caught the light and glistened with scaly crescents of light, as might the restless coils of some great serpent. As the voice of Adamancus chanted louder, it began to take on substance and a semblance of form . . . like Hydra out of myth it was, with many arms instead of many heads, or some malignant Kraken from the vasty deep. Huge it was almost beyond thought, its snaky coils lifting to the vaulted roof . . . and the most horrible thing about the Shape was that it had no face—naught but a blur of mist where a face should be, and yet within this mist two eyes burned forth, like lambent disks of green jade fire, hang-ing in misty vacancy. . . .

The magician ended and hurled his arms aloft in a black ecstasy of worship, head thrown back, eyes rapt on the coiling Thing, frozen in a position of command——

And then the world exploded!

So many things happened so swiftly, event piled upon event, that Sumia, dazed and half entranced by the glim-mering of the Hell Flame and the cold, burning eyes of the Thing From Beyond, could hardly comprehend the sequence of events.

With a thunderous clangor, like hollow worlds colliding, the wall of the chamber shattered to great fragments of black glass, bursting inwards upon the room, hanging in midair like something suspended in a dream. The chamber shook; the very tower reeled on its stony base, as the glittering silvery prow of Thongor's airboat clove through the riven black glass wall and thrust amongst them!

Adamancus uttered a great cry, and staggered back from the falling ruin of his wall . . . and in so doing, he stepped across the circle of phosphorescent light that guarded him from the awful Thing he had summoned from Beyond. . . .

The cold jade eyes of the Thing of a sudden blazed scarlet with an intolerable lust of hunger. Vaporous arms of ophidian smoke uncoiled lazily, and curled about the wizard's stiff, frozen figure. . . .

Through the transparent coils that clasped him, Sumia could see his face, stark white, lips parted in a silent scream, eyes empty and lost, staring from some frigid hell beyond human endurance. The glowing protective talismans upon his person flashed once, arcing with Power, then sizzled out before the clammy embrace of the Hell-Thing.

There was a silent explosion of crimson light.

The flame that burned upon the altar of black emerald flared up, casting rays of scarlet fury to the roof as it exploded, free of the enchanter's control. Hungrily, the writhing flames began to devour the altar, and spread across the floor to envelope the throne-chair and the podium whereon stood the great book of magic spells. The Hell Flame burned without sound, consuming all it touched, and gave off neither heat nor smoke in the fury of its supernatural conflagration.

The spell broken, the vaporous Thing retreated into its strange half-world, bearing with it the frozen body of Adamancus. He *dwindled* from view in some odd manner that cannot quite be explained . . . shrinking as if he receded into limitless distance with inconceivable swiftness.

Then he was gone, as well as the Elemental he had conjured from the nether pits. Only empty air remained.

Half fainting from the shock, Sumia sagged, and fell to the base of the pillar of vitreous blackness. The invisible chains that had bound her against the glassy stalagmite had snapped into nothingness the instant the magician had been seized in the clutches of the Devil-Thing. Shangoth, too, was free. He stepped away from the pillar, avoiding the swift-spreading rush of scarlet flames from the incandescent altar.

Thongor sprang from the prow of the airboat, and seized up Sumia's slim form in his mighty arms. Crushing her against his broad chest, he kissed her fiercely. Her silken lashes fluttered. Color flooded her wan cheeks and pale lips as consciousness returned. She awoke to find herself clasped in the strong arms of the man she loved, feeling the beating of his heart against her own.

"My warrior . . . !" she sighed, lips burning with his kisses.

"My princess!" he replied quietly.

Shangoth came up to them, and Thongor turned from Sumia. Supporting her by one arm that encircled her narrow waist, he extended his other to clasp the blue-skinned giant warmly on the shoulder.

"You, I know, are Shangoth the son of Jomdath," he rumbled, grinning.

The Nomad saluted him. "And you are the great warrior, Thongor of the West," the Rmoahal replied.

Thongor nodded. "Come. My craft awaits. I will take you to your kingly sire, who awaits your coming amid his people in the dead city of Althaar. They hail him as their lord and chief again, and your enemy, the shaman, is undone and overthrown."

"My thanks to you, Thongor. I have no doubt that it was you who were responsible for saving him from his enemies and restored him to his place again, for which no words of mine, however deeply felt, can adequately repay your efforts. But this axe, which I lay at your feet, will strive to repay the great debt I owe unto you!"

Thongor grinned, and clapped him on the shoulder.

"Your debts are paid, and that thrice over, warrior . . . for I, in turn, have no doubt that your strong arm has stood between my princess and many perils ere this hour! But, come—we must board the floater and be off, lest these magic flames engulf us."

A few moments later, the airboat quitted the black tower and rose into the sky. Below it, a sheet of crimson flame swiftly enveloped the bastion of Adamancus from base to cloven crest. The tower of glass burned like a great torch, lighting the barren countryside for many miles about. Seething white amidst the crimson envelope, it crumpled with magic swiftness into a feathery, impalpable dust, falling in silent ruin, the flames consuming it even as it fell.

The storm was over; the great golden moon of primordial Lemuria emerged from the tattered clouds and lit the great plains of the east with her mellow light.

Swiftly and silently the airboat sped towards the north, hurtling like a great silver arrow to the ruined city of Althaar, where Jomdath, Lord of the Jegga Nomads, waited to greet his princely son, and to reward the heroic outlander who had saved them both from a terrible death.

Chapter 16

BLACK DRAGONS VICTORIOUS

Come! raise our song against the sky!
The great Hawk Banner—lift it high!
Our line holds firm—an iron wall,
It is the foe who faint and fall,
  —So let the trumpets call!
  —*Battle-Song of the Black Dragons*

"Release your catapults!"

The command of Hajash Tor rang loud and clear against the evening's silence. The black sky above was suddenly filled with rank after hurtling rank of glittering airboats. They were so numerous, they seemed to fill the heavens from horizon to horizon, soaring majestically forwards towards the great stone walls of Tsargol by the thundering sea.

Like some giant of fable with a thousand arms, the ranged row of catapults lifted into the air, hurling aloft the great fragile globes of delicate glass they had held cupped. The spheres arced into the air and shattered against the hulls of the mighty armada.

As each crystal orb burst, it released a shimmering cloud of dust so powdery and fine that they floated like wreaths of smoke, curling around the flying craft.

From whatever rare mineral the powder had been ground, none save Hajash Tor knew. But the flying dust clouds glowed with a weird silver radiance, like mists of purest light.

The Patangan warriors peered curiously over the rails of the airboats, noting this strange phenomenon. For one long moment, the phosphorescent dust motes shone so

149

brilliantly and were so thick about the keels of the float-ers, that they seemed to be a fleet of magic ships sailing some enchanted see of liquid fire.

In the next instant, the glowing dust-clouds were gone. The silvery urlium hulls of the aerial navy had absorbed the scintillant dust as dry sponges soak up water.

From the flagship, Karm Karvus stared down at the massed forces of Patanga. He could not explain the mys-terious phenomenon of the unknown dust, but he felt obscurely troubled. Something, some ghostly warning, seemed, seemed to clamor against his unhearing senses. Some danger lurked within those radiant clouds of vapor-ous luminance . . . but what?

The answer came but moments later.

The flagship went sluggish. It seemed no longer to re-spond to the sensitive controls. Its prow drifted idly, and the craft began to sink earthwards at an alarming rate. One of Karm Karvus' pilots wrestled futilely with the con-trols, then lifted a tense face to the Prince of Tsargol.

"We are sinking rapidly, Daotar! The lifting-power of the airboat seems somehow impaired."

"Impaired?" rumbled Lord Mael, restively. "How can that be?"

Ald Turmis, Sark of Shembis, pointed through the cabin windows towards the next ship in line with them. "Look!"

They followed his pointing finger, and saw with aston-ishment that the silvery glimmering hue of the urlium hull was darkening; the mirror-bright finish of the magic metal had become dull!

Prince Dru tightened his jaw grimly. "Gentlemen, it seems we are to fight on the ground after all! This Tsar-golian commander has knowledge of some secret regard-ing the manufacture of the magic weightless metal un-known to us. In some manner I cannot fathom, the glow-ing dust he hurled against our fleet has cancelled the lift-ing-power of our fleet!"

Stout old Selverus cursed sulphurously, as did Barand

Thon, Sark of Thurdis. But Zad Komis, Lord of the Black Dragons, wasted no precious moments on giving voice to the consternation and dismay this information caused. He lifted the great battle-horn that hung at his hip and sounded it. The keen call of the horn cut through the evening air, causing his warriors to spring to alertness.

"Black Dragons—*Ho!*"

As the airboats drifted below the tree-tops, the warriors of the Black Dragons vaulted over the rail of their ships and hit the turf, springing up with their long terrible spears at the ready. Advance troops of Tsargol raced towards them, but the Dragons drove the hooked barbs of their war spears into the forward warriors and wreaked terrible slaughter in the first few moments of the battle. Soon, however, more units moved up on foot, surrounding the Black Dragons and cutting them off. And now Hajash Tor's bugles were ringing, summoning mounted warriors from his host. Swift-footed kroters bore the crack fighting-men of Tsargol into action against the unmounted and out-numbered Dragons.

But the Patangan Archers were still aboard the sinking airboats of the fleet, and at a command from Prince Dru, their Daotar, they unlimbered their terrible bows and bent them against the oncoming kroters. They swept the mounted warriors with a withering rain of arrows, and in moments the ranks were all in turmoil, a whirling chaos of bucking kroters, fleeing men, and staggering wounded.

Ald Turmis' determined voice rang out over the noise.

"Thurdans—forward! Cut your way to the Black Dragons!"

The battle was joined in full force. Before many minutes had sped, the warriors of Patanga, Shembis and Thurdis had caught up to the Black Dragons, and spearheaded by the warriors in black, were cutting deep into the mass of Tsargolian soldiery, who were still being swept by blasts from the Patangan bowmen who remained behind on the airboats to take fullest advantage of their height.

But the ships were losing altitude fast. Some ran amok, crashing into the taller trees. Others were carried by vagrant gusts of wind away from the main fleet, coming to earth amidst the enemy. For those gallant warriors, marooned among the foe, let it be said that they fought bravely and to the last man, standing back to back and heaping the slain foe about them as a wall.

It was utter chaos, fighting in the black of night. Even Hajash Tor could see that Tsargolian could not tell friend from foe amidst the darkness, and soon his great trumpets sounded the signal to retreat and reform lines, and the two hosts withdrew. By now all of the Patangan navy had reached earth, and all troops were on foot. And here, of course, the host of Tsargol had the distinct advantage, for many of them were mounted on kroterback, and others on the great war zamphs. Something must be done—and swiftly—to offset this disadvantage.

The fleet had drifted to earth on a rise of ground, and as soon as Zad Komis had time to swiftly appraise their situation, he gathered the host of The Three Cities together and occupied the crest of the low hill. It was a small advantage, but better than nothing; the Tsargolians would have to charge up the slope towards them. The foe would not be able to do so at much speed, and they would be hampered by insecure footing, while on the hillcrest, the warriors of Patanga could stand surefooted, striking downwards at the advancing men. Karm Karvus gave the command to the forward line to lock shields and repel the host when it drove forward to break their line. And then they waited in silence for Hajash Tor to strike.

The canny Daotarkon struck soon. Rather than sending his warriors up against the shield-wall, he set loose the great war zamphs and drove them up the hill against the Patangans. Squealing thunderously, maddened with arrows and spear-thrusts, the gigantic beasts broke the line at a dozen places, and trampled many brave warriors to death before they were slain.

Then the warriors of Tsargol were directed against these broken places in the wall, and soon the very concept of holding a line was lost in the roiling knots of struggling men. The great golden moon of Lemuria shone free from a clear sky by now, and its light was of considerable aid in telling enemy from friend, but the battle's loss seemed a foregone conclusion, even to bold Zad Komis.

Nevertheless, they fought. And each in the private places of his own heart, determined to go down fighting to the very last, rather than yield to the accursed Druids of the Blood-God, on whose terrible altars they would perish ignobly, they knew, were they fools enough to surrender.

Karm Karvus caught but confused and momentary glimpses of his comrades as he fought through the weird golden moonlight that flooded the hill. He saw great Mael shouting some barbarous war song as he laid about him mightily with a twenty-pound bronze hammer. The old Baron, stout and short of breath though he was, smashed men aside with his hammer-strokes as if they were but toys, and when he vanished from Karm Karvus' sight he was still battering about him lustily.

Prince Dru, no longer the languid, foppish courtier who sauntered from gaming table to boudoir with an ironic jest or dainty verse on his lips, fought with the cold ferocity of a tiger, howling curses as his deadly rapier flashed like a needle of brilliant light, slashing from throat and arm and unprotected breast. The languid prince displayed the prowess of a magnificent swordsman. When Karm Karvus last caught a glimpse of him, he held three Tsargolians at sword-point, having slain two others of the five who had assaulted him.

The others he could not see, although he guessed that Ald Turmis, surrounded by a ring of his faithful Shemban swordsmen, was holding the crest of the hill . . . and somewhere down the further slope, Zad Komis and old Baron

Selverus had pulled together a large number of Black Dragons, and led them through the massed enemy to the rescue of a band of archers near the edge of the woods who, unarmed with swords, were at the mercy of the Tsargolians. These bowmen Zad Komis saved from certain death and directed to climb the trees, wherefrom, with the vantage of height, they fired decisive volleys of arrows into the Tsargolians through the rest of the long, weary battle.

After an endless time, the foe withdrew, and Zad Komis joined Karm Karvus on the slope. They were too exhausted to follow up this chance and pursue the fleeing Tsargolians, and seized this opportunity to rest. Karm Karvus organized a number of footsoldiers and bade them search for water and wine in the grounded floaters, passing these drinkables along to the other warriors. They then waited quietly for Hajash Tor to reform his lines and charge the hill again.

Again and again through the weary hours of this unending night, the massed might of Tsargol went up against the hill; each time they were thrown back, but each time by a slimmer margin of strength. Karm Karvus' sword arm grew so weary it became numb. He lost all count of the pattern of combat . . . the battle became for him nothing more than a noisy waking dream wherein howling, sweat-smeared and dusty faces swam up before him to be cut down, with other such faces swimming up through a red haze to replace those that fell at his feet in red ruin. . . .

And then, it seemed, the world went mad.

Suddenly, everyone was gaping above them, staring at the eastern sky. With a distinct shock, Karm Karvus saw the east was red with dawn, and they knew they must have fought all through the long night. But what of the dawn—why were all the warriors staring at it open-mouthed?

Then his bleary vision cleared, and with it suddenly a great rush of hope lifted his heart. For there, soaring out of the unknown east, came a sleek airboat, glittering in the brilliance of dawn.

It swooped down over the battlefield and hovered above the center of the Tsargolian host, where the commanders of the enemy were clustered. And down from its deck swarmed a fantastic host of monstrous warriors, blue-skinned giants who stood nine feet tall in their barbaric, jewel-encrusted trappings, and wielded terrible bronze axes of tremendous weight in their gigantic hands.

They struck like a thunderbolt into the very heart of the enemy host. Hajash Tor was gaping at the sky when Shangoth of the Nomads dropped down beside him like some warrior god from the skies. The Prince of the Jegga grinned, and great muscles bunched along his giant shoulders. His great war ax whistled through the air, and the severed head of Hajash Tor went bouncing among his warriors, gushing a flood of gore.

Jugrim and Chundja and other Jegga warriors of the prince's retinue who had accompanied him in Thongor's floater, swung down from the rails of the hovering floater and dropped amidst the astounded enemy. A dozen noble Daotars of the Tsargolian host, paralyzed with awe at the apparition of these indigo ogres from the sky, died in the first few instants. The great bronze axes lifted and fell, and lifted again, streaming with crimson.

Arzang Pome, the toadlike ex-Sark of Shembis, fell scrambling from his mount as his zamph went mad at the strange new odor of the Rmoahal giants. He shrieked once, as the mighty three-toed paw of the rearing zamph came down upon his head . . . and never again did the sadistic little Sark make a sound, at least in this life.

As his Rmoahals cut a red path through the command post of the Tsargolians, Thongor himself appeared, his broadsword in his hand, and as he vaulted over the rail, the weary warriors of Patanga and Shembis and Thurdis gave out with a stupendous, earth-shaking shout of triumph.

155

*"Hai—*Thonger! THONGOR!"

Numadak Quelm, fanatic young priest of Yamath, was hauled spitting like a cat from his mount by Thongor's massive hand—and died, with two feet of clean Valkarthan steel through his viperish heart.

Within seconds, the center of the Tsargolian host was a seething chaos of running, shouting, dying men. The great bronze war axes of the Rmoahal, as heavy as a man and even taller, swung by all the fantastic strength of those nine-foot warriors, clove through steel armor and shield and helm as if they were thin paper. A backhanded stroke in the capable hands of Thongor's great friend, Shangoth, hewed three Tsargolian warriors down and clove through the pole to which the war banner of Tsargol was affixed, bringing the mighty standard down in the dust.

At this, as at the death of their leaders, the Tsargolians lost heart.

And this was the chance Karm Karvus and Zad Komis needed. They assaulted the Tsargolian line, charging down their hill, and weariness left their limbs at the sight of Thongor. It was as if they had slept all night, instead of fighting. A deep chanted war song burst from the lips of the Black Dragons as they crashed like so many iron thunderbolts into the rear of the wavering Tsargolian line. Their red swords rose and fell and rose again, cutting a crimson track through the press of struggling men. Where before through the busy hours of the night they had fought like men, now they fought like devils, and flesh and blood could not stand before their irresistible charge.

The Tsargolian line broke in a thousand places. Thongor and a dozen giant Rmoahal warriors wrought red ruin in the heart and center of the host, while the hordes of Patanga and Sembis and Thurdis smote all along the front of their position. Like men ground between two millstones, they *broke.* Thousands threw down their arms and fled in every direction, seeking to get away from the grinning hordes of the Black Dragon, from the flashing axes of the blue giants, and from the crimson sword of Thongor the Unconquerable.

They did not get far. The keen-eyed Patangan Archers had invested the crest of the hill, and swept them with a stinging rain of death-dealing arrows.

Thus fell Tsargol, and the West was saved.

＊

> And Thongor lifted his hand and broke the iron walls of Tsargol by the sea, and uprooted from all that land the Cult of Slidith the Red, sending forth into exile all they that worshipped him; and Thongor set over the peoples of the coast his comrade, Karm Karvus, as their Sark, and the Empire of The Three Cities became great over all the West, and The Three Cities became Four, and lo! the Gods were pleased. . . .
>
> Thus sayeth *The Lemurian Chronicles*.

GREAT SCIENCE FICTION
FROM WARNER BOOKS

MEANWHILE
by Max Handley   (87-643, $5.95)

From the depths of the ocean a man emerges onto a world devoid of males for centuries. A stunning, illustrated science fiction novel that signals the emergence of a major new talent.

A CITY IN THE NORTH
by Marta Randall   (94-062, $1.75)

They set out to discover the secrets of the dead among the ruins—and found, instead, the secret of their survival.

FALSE DAWN
by Chelsea Quinn Yarbro   (90-077, $1.95)

In the 21st Century, mutant is a dirty word. Thea is a mutant, despised, feared, and marked for death. Then a mutilated male appears and their survival hinges on their love.

THE PHILOSOPHER'S STONE
by Colin Wilson   (89-442, $1.95)

A prophetic novel whose premise is "that man must come into active conscious control of his own brain, or the species will become extinct."

THE BEST OF JUDITH MERRIL
by Judith Merril   (86-058, $1.25)

A collection of the best works of science fiction by the pioneering feminist, activist author whose stories reflect penetrating studies into the psyche of the women of the future.

MORE GREAT SCIENCE FICTION

THOSE GENTLE VOICES
by George Alec Effinger   (94-017, $1.75)
What will happen when men from Earth encounter other intelligent forms of life—a race so primitive it hadn't even discovered the spear, or fire . . .

WHEN WORLDS COLLIDE
by Philip Wylie and Edwin Balmer
                              (89-971, $1.95)
When the extinction of Earth is near, scientists build rocket ships to evacuate a chosen few to a new planet. But the secret leaks out and touches off a savage struggle among the world's most powerful men for the million-to-one chance of survival.

AFTER WORLDS COLLIDE
by Philip Wylie and Edwin Balmer
                              (89-974, $1.95)
The startling sequel to WHEN WORLDS COLLIDE. Survivors of Earth on Bronson Beta realize they are not the only humans alive—and learn the other group is out to destroy them.

ON WHEELS
by John Jakes   (89-932, $1.95)
Automotive revolution has finally overrun human evolution in this vision of the future where to drop below 40 mph means certain death.

THX-1138
by Ben Bova   (89-711, $1.95)
Visit the future where love is the ultimate crime. Meet the nameless man who dares to pit himself against the state. STAR WARS director-author George Lucas's original story of man's war for humanity in the 25th century.

GREAT SCIENCE FICTION FROM WARNER...

A CITY IN THE NORTH
by Marta Randall   (94-062, $1.75)

They are set out to discover the secrets of the dead among the ruins — and found, instead, the secret of their survival.

THE BEST OF JUDITH MERRIL
by Judith Merril   (86-058, $1.25)

A collection of the best works of science fiction by the pioneering, feminist, activist author whose stories reflect penetrating studies into the psyche of the women of the future.

THOSE GENTLE VOICES
by George Alec Effinger   (94-017, $1.75)

What will happen when men from Earth encounter other intelligent forms of life — a race so primitive it hadn't even discovered the spear, or fire . . . .